FRESH

Mark McNay was born in 1956 and brought up in a mining village in central Scotland. After a failed electrical engineering course and fifteen years doing odd jobs, Mark joined the UEA creative writing course in 1999. He graduated in 2003 with distinction. *Fresh* is his first novel, and won the Arts Foundation New Fiction Award 2007.

FRESH

MARK
MCNAY

CANONGATE

Edinburgh · London · New York · Melbourne

For my brothers, Brian and wee Skell

First published in Great Britain in 2007 by
Canongate Books Ltd, 14 High Street,
Edinburgh EH1 1TE

This paperback edition first published in 2008 by
Canongate Books

1

British Library Cataloguing-in-Publication Data
A catalogue record for this book is available on
request from the British Library

ISBN 978 1 84767 082 3

Typeset in Bembo by
Palimpsest Book Production Limited,
Grangemouth, Stirlingshire

Printed and bound by
Clays Ltd, St Ives plc

www.canongate.net

ACKNOWLEDGEMENTS

Thanks are due to the following people and organizations:

The AHRB for financial support that enabled me to write this novel.

Staff and classmates at UEA for constructive criticism.

Andrew Cowan for encouragement and guidance.

Michal Shavit, Georgia Garrett, and Francis Bickmore for reading my drafts and helping to form them into this novel.

CHAPTER 1

The street lights were dimmed by the threat of dawn.
He shivered. His wellies made a hollow scraping sound
as he trudged to the bus stop. He coughed and it echoed
round the pebble-dash of Cadge Road. He picked a bit
of chicken feather from his overalls and let it flutter into
his slipstream.

Alright wee man?

Sean turned and saw Rab and Albert coming out of
the path at the side of Royston Road. He waited for
them.

Alright boys?

His uncle Albert was smoking a roll-up. Rab had his
hands in his pockets and swaggered like boys his age
should. Sean looked at him and thought twelve years in
the factory would take the swing out of his shoulders.

What are ye lookin so cocky about?

It's Friday.

Albert had a final puff and threw his dog-end onto the
pavement. He smiled.

He thinks he's on to a promise the night.

Sean inspected his cousin.

Is that right?

Rab glanced at his dad and back to Sean.

Maybe.

Sean looked at Albert.

It's about time he popped his cherry.

Ah'm no a virgin ya cunt.

Sean looked at Albert and smiled. Then he turned to Rab.

Alright wee man. Ah'm only kiddin with ye.

As long as ye know.

The bus stop had men round it smoking and coughing and spitting. Sean and Albert sat together on the bench. Rab stood next to the other teenagers. They stood in a circle talking about drinking and fighting and fucking. Sean listened to them for a second and turned to his uncle. Albert nodded at the youngsters. Sean gave Albert a resigned look. Sean knew he was getting old because he'd rather sit with his uncle than stand with the boys.

It wasn't meant to be like this. Him and Maggie had some big ideas when they started seeing each other. They could have went to Canada or London, anything but get a house on Cadge Road. Maggie was lovely though. Long dark hair and blue eyes. Best-looking girl in the class. Jammy bastard they used to call him.

Albert touched Sean on the shoulder.

Fag?

Sean took the pouch and made a roll-up. He passed it back and Albert gave him a light.

Are ye for the Fiveways the night? said Albert.

Sean felt gutted.

No.

What again? How no?

Ah've got debts to pay.

Ye must have with all that overtime ye've been puttin in.

Sean had a long puff on his fag.

It's doin my fuckin head in.

So what are ye payin off?

Donna's school trip.

From last year?

It was only six months ago.

Albert chuckled.

Aye time flies when yer old.

Albert smiled.

As long as she enjoyed herself.

Aye she did. But as soon as she got back all Ah heard was Christmas this and Christmas that.

Aye well that's weans for ye.

Innit?

They're dear son but worth it in the long run.

Sean looked at Albert.

Ah fuckin hope so.

Well look at how you turned out. Ye were well worth it.

Thanks Uncle Albert.

And look at our Rab. He'll be alright as well.

Aye but look at our Archie.

Albert shook his head.

There's always one'll turn out rotten.

Ah hope it isnay Donna.

Albert grabbed Sean's knee.

No she's a good lassie. And she's got you and Maggie as examples. She'll be alright.

Ah fuckin hope so.

Ah know what ye need. A wee bit of fun. Take yer mind off all that serious shit that's weighin ye down.

Tell me about it.

So c'mon out for a pint the night.

Ah cannay afford it.

Ye can surely afford one pint.

Sean felt really gutted.

Ah wish Ah could but Ah cannay.

Albert nodded and called to Rab.

D'ye hear that?

What?

Yer cousin's no comin for a pint the night.

Rab gave Sean a pitying look.

That's what marriage does to ye.

Sean stared at the shops across the street from the bus shelter. Albert slapped him on the leg.

Ah don't know how ye do it. Ah'm chokin for a pint now.

Sean smacked his lips.

Tell me about it.

Ah well only ten hours to go eh?

Sean felt miserable.

More like six months.

What are ye talkin about?

That's how long Ah'll be payin this fuckin debt.

How, who d'ye owe?

Sean nearly told but he never. Albert put his hand on his shoulder.

Don't worry young fella, Ah'll buy ye one in the Saracen at lunchtime.

A double-decker appeared at the end of the street. Albert stood up and shouldered his satchel. The younger men dropped their cigarettes and stood on them. They jostled to get on first. Sean got on last, said cheers pal to the driver, and went upstairs to sit with Albert at the front. They didn't say much, just looked out the front window at gangs of workers readying themselves as they approached a stop. The doors hissed open and it got louder as the bus filled up. Before long they were on the dual-carriageway.

The lights up the middle of the carriageway flashed past and made Albert look like someone out of an old film. Then they were out of the city and the lights stopped. They were flying in the dark. The bus slowed and indicated and turned. It rolled up a lane pushing Sean and Albert together then pulling them apart. The engine whimpered as it climbed the gears after every curve. Occasional overhanging branches would clip the side of the bus. Sometimes, through gaps in the trees, Sean would catch a glimpse of the factory, each image larger than the last. Slowly it climbed out of the dark and they were beside it, intimidated. From the top deck it looked like a prison, or a Ministry of Defence establishment. Barbed wire and searchlights and a chimney pumping smoke into the sky. The whine and whirr of machinery and no dawn chorus. The roar of buses coming from all directions. Red buses from the east and orange buses from the west.

Security guards watched as the workers were disgorged from the buses and crowded round the clock shed. Some men pushed forward as if they were eager to get in the factory and on with their work. Sean hung back. He could smell the meat and fat of a million dead chickens. The longer he could stay away from it the better. The crowd started to thin and Sean was pulled through with the stragglers. He nodded to the security guard, punched his card through the clock, and he was a prisoner of the factory. He followed the others to the golden light coming through the door of the building.

Sean walked through the wet corridors towards the cloakroom. On the way he passed mates who'd just finished the night shift. They were smiling and the odd one would wink and nod. Sean tried to smile back but couldn't manage more than a grimace. When he got to the cloakroom, he hung his bag on his peg and went to the toilets with Albert for a smoke.

A white cap was in the toilet combing his hair in the mirror. He carefully put on his hairnet.

Who are ye dressin up for? said Sean to the white cap.

The boy put on his cap.

Nobody, he said.

How long ye been here?

Nine weeks.

Blue cap next week then eh?

The boy looked proud.

Aye.

Albert put his hands in his pockets.

It's no everybody that can stick this shite out for ten weeks.

Ah didnay think Ah'd do it.

Where are ye workin? said Sean.

Portions.

D'ye hear that Albert? Portions.

Albert nodded.

What, for nine weeks? said Sean.

The boy nodded.

Albert and Sean nodded. Impressed.

Yer more of a man than me son.

Albert pulled his cap firmly onto his head.

So how come George put ye in Portions?

Who's George?

The foreman.

Ah thought his name was Malcolm.

It is. Every cunt calls him George but.

The white cap had a final adjustment, straightened his overalls and left the toilet.

Imagine that, nine weeks in Portions. Poor wee cunt, said Sean.

He cannay have a sense of smell.

Sean shuddered. Albert had a draw on his fag and leaned against the wall.

So when are we expectin Archie?

Sean scratched his head and frowned.

It's just over six months to go. Ah think.

D'ye no know?

Aye. Ah got a letter off him at Christmas. He's gettin out in July. But ye know what he's like. He'll probably have a fight with a screw the day before and end up in there for another six months.

Albert laughed.

Aye maybe. But ye'll be pleased to see him anyway.

Tryin to be funny?

7

Albert laughed. Sean didn't. Albert flicked his ash on the floor.

Where will he be stayin when he gets out?

Sean laughed and nodded.

So he'll no be stayin round yours?

What, after the last time? Yer auntie Jessie would kill me if Ah even mentioned his name, never mind ask if he could stay.

Aye, Maggie's the same.

Has he sorted out the drugs?

Ah fuckin hope so. Ah couldnay live through that madness again. Right come on. We better move.

Albert looked at his watch.

Aye. It's ten past already.

They dropped their butts into the urinal with the 'Please do not drop your cigarette ends into the urinals' sign above it, adjusted their blue caps in the mirror, and left the toilet. As they walked into the corridor Sean pulled his gloves on. They got to the double doors at the bottom of the corridor and pushed through them into the expanse that was Fresh.

Sean blinked as his eyes got used to the light. It could have been an aircraft hanger it was so big in there. Lines of chickens looped and crossed below the roof like they were on a giant roller coaster taking them for a fun day out. There were five conveyor belts arranged on the floor where the lines dropped chickens at one end, and women with hats and hairnets hovered above the belts waiting to truss them. Sean and Albert walked through Fresh till they came to a raised section at the end called the Junction. Here the chickens were sorted into those that went to Fresh and those that went to Frozen. The chickens destined for Fresh were sorted by weight and sent to the conveyor belts and packed ready to be sold up and down the country.

Fresh chickens to be sold in butchers and supermarkets for the ease of the purchasing public. Fresh chickens you assume have been killed recently. You picture a redbrick farmyard with purple foxgloves growing in a corner. The healthy smell of shite. An old 1950s tractor quietly rusting on flat tyres, only useful to the robins that nest under the seat. The farmer's wife comes out of the door, pulls a chicken from the ground it was idly pecking, and twists its neck with her fat powerful hands. She sits on a stool, places the quivering bird on her lap, and plucks it while it's warm. She sings a song of somebody's lover lost in a foreign war. She stuffs hand-stitched pillows with the feathers and sells them on the local market on a Wednesday afternoon. The plucked and dressed chicken is trussed ready to be hung that afternoon in the butcher's and you walk in and buy a bird whose pulse has barely died in its throat.

The fresh chickens Sean handles are driven to the factory in shoebox-sized containers packed on the trailer of an articulated truck. The driver flicks a roll-up butt out of the window and calls for Rab, who sidles out of his hut and guides the lorry into the loading bay. Strong forearms reach into the shoeboxes and drag their prey into the artificial light and hang them by the ankles on a hook. They fly along, upside down, flapping their wings, trying to escape, shitting down their chests,

9

squawking and pecking at their mates. The hooks drag them into a tank of water where an electric current stops their hearts moments before rubber wheels grind the feathers from their skin.

By the time they reach Sean they've been eviscerated and beheaded and spent time in a refrigerated still-room where they remain until they cool. They appear from a hole in the wall next to Sean's station and a computer decides whether to drop them or not onto the conveyor belt that flanks the wall. There is a rhythm to the line. Bum-titty-bum-titty-bum-titty.

Sean's breath was smoke-like in the cool air. He was bored. He tried to blow smoke rings but all he got was puffs of steam. He pressed his hand into the conveyor belt to see if he could slow it down, to feel it struggle over the rollers, to change the tone of the machine. He pushed his finger back and forth over the belt to make a flowing pattern in the grease. He spat a green oyster onto the belt and watched it disappear into the distance. He stamped his feet to keep them warm.

*

Ah could hardly keep my eyes open. Every five minutes the teacher would shout O'Grady and Ah would twitch from the window back to the blackboard. About halfway into the lesson the head pushed his face round the door and asked her if he could have a word with me. Ah shat myself coz Ah thought Ah was nabbed for writin he was a wanker on the toilet door. He gave me a right funny look when Ah came into the corridor and Ah nearly telt him how sorry Ah was, but as we walked towards his office Ah saw Archie waitin outside.

We went in and stood across from his desk. He sat down and looked at us. Then he telt us we'd have to be grown up about what he was goin to say. We looked at each other and back at him and nodded. Our ma had been ran down by a coal lorry on the Petershill Road. She was in the Royal Infirmary and her condition was grave. He got up and took us into his typist's office. She gave us a sweetie each and we sat down and waited while the head tried to get our uncle. Archie picked a massive snotter out his nose and showed me it before he wiped it under his chair.

About half an hour later my uncle Albert came into the school and took us round to his. He said the hospital was no place for weans and the best place for us was with our auntie Jessie. So we sat at the kitchen table eatin cakes and tea and he went to the hospital to visit my ma. By the time he got home that night we were in our beds. He woke us up to tell us our ma had took a turn for the worse. We didnay know what to say. Archie looked at me for a while then he turned his head and went back to sleep. Well Ah thought he did but years later he telt me he waited till he heard my breathin go, then he fell asleep himself.

The next mornin my auntie Jessie said we could have the day off and Ah thought brilliant. But my uncle Albert turned round and said we'd need somethin to keep our minds off our ma so he sent us in. It was alright. People kept askin me if it was true my ma was dead. Ah got extra puddin at school dinners as well. And about halfway through the afternoon my uncle Albert came in for us and took us to Pat's cafe.

He sat us down in the window seat and went and got us a Coke and a KitKat each. Then he put his hand on Archie's arm and telt us that he'd always looked at us as just the sort of boys him and my auntie Jessie wished they had themselves. We were strong boys and our ma and da would be proud of us. Me and Archie chewed our KitKats and nodded. Then he telt us. Our ma was dead but we werenay to worry coz we were coming to live with him. Archie got up and ran out. Ah just sat there and finished my KitKat.

The polis brought Archie back three days later. He had a black eye. They said they'd had to restrain him and it took three of them to get him in the motor. They'd found him down the Central Station trying to jump on a train to London. Just like yer da said my uncle Albert, and patted Archie on the head. He gave Archie a cuddle and smiled at my auntie Jessie. Ah've never saw my uncle look so sad. No even when we went to the funeral.

*

A flurry of dead birds brought Sean back to the factory. O'Grady banged those chickens on the line. One after the other. Bang. Bang. Bang. And here we are in the final of the Embassy world chicken-hanging competition at the Crucible in Sheffield. And what a competition it's been. O'Grady has struggled to find his form this year and there have been times when we doubted he'd make it into the final. But make it he did and what a game he's given Hendry. Both players have had opportunities to win, but neither of them have fully exploited their chances. In the last frame we thought O'Grady had lost but Hendry missed an easy three-pounder and gave the frame away. And here we are in the final frame. Two chickens left to go and the pressure is on. O'Grady needs to hang the pair of them to win. He reaches for the first chicken, and look at this, he's flashing a smile at the crowd, does this man feel no pressure? Listen to them cheer. No wonder they call him the chicken-hanger of the people. The crowd is going wild. Hang them chickens they chant. But O'Grady lets them drift towards the end of the line and the long drop to the floor. Fifty thousand pounds hang in the balance. What is he doing? The chickens are turning and tumbling from the end of the line when O'Grady catches them in mid-air and slams them home. What a hero.

CHAPTER 2

His belly rumbled.

Ah'm fuckin starvin.

If it went on much longer they'd turn up and he'd be sat in the corner, grey and dead from malnutrition. Like a fucking skeleton he'd be. All sucked in at the cheekbones, with a bit of a beard and spiders' webs hanging from his chin. Clumps of hair missing from his head like some pensioner with leukaemia. Loose teeth stuck in his skin where he'd been gnawing at his fingers. Knees twice as wide as his thighs. He'd have a beer belly like them kids from Ethiopia. He'd have dead eyes and bluebottles crawling over his face, in and out of his mouth, laying eggs on him to hatch into maggots and chew him up. Before he was dead, even. They'd be eating out through his eyes, and in his nose, and saying die you bastard, that one's for our Charlie, he was only five days old when you pulled his legs off. And the rats would come out and nibble through his wellies until they could get at his toes, his delicious toes, crunched on like spare ribs from the Chinese with that lovely sauce and sitting on a bed of lettuce.

When he went for break he'd start with a packet of

salt and vinegar crisps. Tangy and crunchy and just enough to get the digestion going for the cheese sandwiches. Cheese sandwiches. A nice piece of soft white bread, fresh out the freezer, chewy and slowly releasing the flavoursome cheddar cheese Maggie gets from the Co-op. Washed down with a lovely cup of stewed tea. Nice. Then for afters, a Tunnock's milk chocolate caramel wafer, over 4,000,000 sold every week.

C'mon ya bastards Ah'm dyin for my fuckin dinner. Them cunts in evisceration had theirs ages ago.

Sean jumped up and down on the spot. Two-footed jumps alternated with little skips. Bum titty jump joggy bum titty jump joggy. After a period of warm-up exercises he started grunting through his nose and jabbing with his left. Jab jab jab. Then he moved on to the complete workout. Bum titty left left-right bum titty left left-right. The world champion was limbering up to take on yet another contender. How many fights has he had this year? Word from his training camp is his confidence has never been this good. According to his manager he is peaking at just the right moment and the training team are convinced he will still be the world champion this time tomorrow. Let's have a look at the champion and we can see for ourselves how confident this man is.

He ducked and jabbed at the chickens as they passed him on the line. When a bird came he followed it down the line giving it left left-right. The bang on the fat breast had just enough give to make it feel like a human cheek. Sometimes the punch knocked a bit of fat out that looked like a tooth. Sometimes it was just a spray of water like the saliva from a punched mouth. Mostly it was just the satisfaction of getting the timing right. Send it out with the jabs and bang it hard with the right when it was swinging back. Knuckles deep into the flesh. Lovely. It was like practice for Friday night and they were paying him five quid an hour for it. Nice work if ye can get it.

The rhythm changed and the chickens came down faster and faster. Sean found it hard to catch up and they piled like corpses in the rain. As he tried to pick one up another would bounce off the back of his hand. Sometimes their legs, or shorn feet, would dig him right in the finger. It was like when you're in a fight and the guy gets a couple in. You need to go like fuck even though you think it's all over. Keep pluggin away as his father used to say. Never let them win easy, then even if you lose they'll leave you alone because there are softer targets. And it wasn't going to be easy with these bastards. It felt like every time you grabbed a chicken by the leg, dragged it from the tangle of bodies, four of its buddies had taken its place. The pile threatened to bury him but the thought of Albert telling the other lads at break how he couldn't manage his line made Sean catch a rhythm and steam through those chickens like Ali steaming Foreman. His hands moved like lightning. He gave them so many punches they thought they were surrounded. So many lefts they were begging for a right. The round finished and the champion was still undisputed and undefeated.

★

We'd only been stayin with Albert and Jessie for two weeks when we started at St Roch's. Ah didnay like it. Ah didnay know anybody. Everybody else was goin about in gangs laughin and talkin and that. A lot of the older guys were smokin and havin dummy fights. Ah just kept my gub shut and tried to get through the day without gettin a batterin.

Ah got home that night and my uncle Albert asked me how was school. Never mind son he said when Ah telt him. Ye'll soon settle in. He telt Archie to make sure Ah was alright. Archie said if anybody gave me any shite just to tell him and he'd sort them out. Albert laughed and said right enough son tell yer brother if ye get any shite. My auntie wasnay so pleased. She telt Albert to stop encouragin Archie to get into fights. They're lads Jessie, he said, ye've got to expect the odd bit of fisticuffs. Is that no right son? he said, and slapped Archie on the side of the head. Archie tried to duck but he wasnay quick enough for Albert. Well no yet anyway.

Archie said he liked the school. There was some nice lookin lassies. Albert said he didnay want any trouble at the door and him and Archie had a laugh. My auntie said that was terrible and what are they like. She smiled at me. We ate our tea and my uncle went to the Fiveways. Archie went to the youth club. Me and Jessie watched the telly and Ah did my homework.

The next day at school Ah was waitin in the queue for dinners and this third year pushed in front of me. Ah asked him what he thought he was playin at. There's a line ye know. He gave me a look and asked me what the fuck Ah was goin to do about it. Ah looked at the floor and said nothin. He was a bit bigger than what Ah'd thought. When Ah was eatin my dinner he sat next to me. He pushed his finger up his nose. Then he stuck it in my puddin. He asked if Ah was goin to eat it. Ah let him have it. Ah didnay want any of his bugs.

At tea that night my auntie was pleased coz Ah seemed ravenous. My uncle laughed and said the O'Grady boys had big appetites Ah thought ye'd know that by now Jessie. Archie dropped his cutlery, wiped his mouth and left the kitchen sayin he was goin out. Albert said he was goin to the Fiveways. My auntie said Ah should go out as well. It's no good for a lad to be sittin in with his old auntie every night. Ah went into the street and had a game of football. Ah was a good goalie. When Ah was goin back indoors John Gambol said see ye the morra Sean and waved.

The next mornin Gambo called for me on the way to school. My auntie telt him to come in and asked if he wanted a drink of juice. He said no thanks. She asked if he wanted a biscuit. He said no thanks. She asked if he was sure. My uncle said she was embarrassin the boy. When we were walkin down the Cadge Road Gambo said my auntie and uncle were nice. We got to the Fiveways roundabout and Ah saw the guy who ate my puddin. He was with a gang of smokers. Gambo telt me it was Sammy McCann and Ah should steer clear. Nothin but trouble. Best if he doesnay even notice ye. Ah didnay tell Gambo about the puddin. Ah didnay want him to think Ah was a prick.

Sammy spotted me as we were passin but. He started

callin me an immigrant. Me and my family should fuck off back where we came from. Ah kept my eyes down and tried to ignore him. Gambo gave me a funny look but he walked beside me. Ah'll always remember that. Then when we were almost past Sammy threw an empty can at me and it caught me right on the ear. Ah rubbed my ear and kept walkin.

That was the start of it. My dinners were ate without the puddin. Somebody put chewin gum in my hair. Somebody put a lit fag doubt in the hood of my parka. Ah got in from school and my auntie Jessie noticed the fag burn. She went mental. Asked me if Ah'd been smokin. Ah said no. She smelled my breath and my fingers. Then she asked how that happened. Ah telt her Ah didnay know. She didnay believe me. When my uncle came in Ah was called into the kitchen for a wee talk. He asked me what was goin on. Ah said nothin. He telt me the only way to deal with bullies was to pick out the biggest one and kick fuck out of him. Every bully's a shitebag son. Stand up to them and they'll back down. OK uncle Albert, Ah said. But Ah wasnay convinced and he knew it.

He shouted for Archie and telt my auntie Jessie he was takin the boys down the Fiveways. She wasnay too happy. Ah think she knew what was goin to happen. Watch yerself Albert that McGrory isnay as daft as he looks, as we left the house. Typical woman boys, if they're no worryin about one thing they're worryin about another. Archie laughed and said aye Ah know.

On the way down he telt us about McGrory. The cunt had borrowed a tenner off my uncle and telt him to get to fuck when he asked for it back. Albert wouldnay have put up with that shite if it wasnay for the fact that McGrory was with his pals and Albert was with my auntie Jessie.

We piled through the doors of the pub and it went a bit quiet. The barman gied me a funny look. Ah was only eleven. But my uncle asked if he had a problem with the wee boy and the barman shook his head and started pourin my uncle a pint of Guinness. Albert leaned his elbow on the bar and gied his five o'clock shadow a rasp as he looked round the bar. One twenty-five said the barman. And two halves of lager for the boys. Ah cheered up at that. Archie asked for fifty pence for the bandit and my uncle growled and telt him he was pushin his luck.

He paid the barman and gied us our drinks and we went to a table. The lager tasted rotten but Ah couldnay let him down so Ah sipped it and telt him it was grand. He smiled his tight smile and had a swallow of the Guinness. Then he rolled a roll-up and asked us who we thought was the biggest guy in the bar. Archie pointed to a guy at the end of the bar who had three mates with him. Albert took a swallow and nodded. He wiped his lips with the back of his hand. Aye boys that's McGrory the cheeky cunt.

He got up and telt us to look and learn. Archie rubbed his hands the gether and nudged me in the ribs. Ah farted. My uncle approached the wee team and started talkin to them. Ah saw McGrory eyein him up but Albert was kiddin on he'd hardly noticed him. The guy's pals spread out a bit. They knew what was comin and didnay want to get caught in the middle.

It didnay take long for the fireworks to start. It was raised voices and pointin at each other. Ah could see McGrory's face get a bit red. Then he flung a right hook and Albert ducked, took the hook on the side of the head and got two digs under the guy's ribs. Then he was up straight, two lefts into the face followed by a hard right and the guy went down like a sack of shite.

McGrory went into a wee huddle on the floor and my uncle gied him a few hard boots in the guts. Where's my fuckin tenner? he shouted. Then he bent down and grabbed the front of his tee shirt and shook him. Where's my fuckin tenner? As he done this McGrory put his hands in his back pocket and pulled out a wad. My uncle grabbed the money and pushed McGrory to the floor. His head made a hollow crack as it hit the tiles. Albert peeled a tenner off the wad and threw the rest in McGrory's face.

He walked back to the table kissin a split on his knuckles, sat down and had a big swig of beer. See what Ah mean boys he said. We nodded. He swallowed the rest of his pint and went up to the bar for another. The barman said it was on the house. Albert sat down and had a couple of drinks. He rolled a fag and telt us a coward dies a thousand deaths but a hero only dies the once. His eyes were sparklin when he telt us that. Then he went for a piss and Archie said that was fuckin brilliant wait till Ah tell the boys about this. McGrory was at the bar bein comforted by his mates. Where were ye? he was sayin to them. They just shook their heads.

The next mornin Archie said he'd walk in to school with me and Gambo. Ah didnay want him to. Last thing Ah wanted was our Archie bein confronted with how much of a shitebag his wee brother was. Sammy noticed Archie and he hesitated but his pals were there so he didnay have a choice. Where's yer skirt ye Springburn homo? he shouted. Archie looked at me and looked at Sammy as if he couldnay believe what he was hearin. What did ye say ya cunt? he said. Fuck off back where ye belong said Sammy. Archie was across the road and over the railins as fast as fuck. Sammy blinked and tried to mingle with his mates but Archie was havin none of that. Ah saw his head flash and Sammy was reelin back till he bounced off a fence. He put up a good fight but Archie was too strong for him and it wasnay long before Sammy was on the deck. Archie gave him a kick in the guts and told him to pick on guys his own size in future. Then he turned to Sammy's pals and asked if any of them wanted some. They shook their heads. Gambo couldnay believe it but he'd never saw Archie in action before. That's how ye deal with bullies Archie said as he wiped Sammy's blood off his forehead. Just attack the cunts.

Later on at school Sammy came up to me in the dinner hall and asked me to shake his hand. No hard feelins he said. Ah just shook my head. Ah didnay know what to say. Me and Gambo shrugged at each other and finished our dinner. Gambo said he wished he had a brother like Archie. We put our plates on the tray and walked into the playground. Archie and Sammy were in the middle of a gang of lads showin them the details of the mornin's fight. Archie said Sammy had some fuckin left hook. Sammy laughed and said fuckin right Ah have. After a coupla weeks the two of them were best pals.

CHAPTER 3

The cloakroom was full of guys sitting on benches munching sandwiches out of Tupperware boxes. Sean went to the sink and gave his hands a good wash. Then he picked up his bag and sat between two guys. It was a bit tight so he wiggled his arse to make more room. They tutted but they moved. Sean pulled his box out of his bag and opened it. He threw one of the bags of crisps over to Albert.

Thanks son.

No bother old yin.

Not a lot was said in the cloakroom. The men were too busy cramming their food into their mouths so they would have time for a fag before they had to go back to the chickens. Sean ate the crisps and the sandwiches and he was halfway through his chocolate biscuit before he realised he had missed the break. He always meant to take his time. Savour the fifteen minutes as if they were finely spiced steak slices. But it never happened. He munched through his food and didn't even taste it half the time. One minute his box was full and the next he was putting the lid on and pushing it back into his bag.

Sean finished the chocolate biscuit and made a ball out of the wrapper. He flicked it at a white cap and looked away. The white cap had a look around and Sean caught his eye and pointed to Albert. The white cap threw a bit of bread at Albert. The old guy pointed to the white cap.

What the fuck are ye playin at?

The white cap went red and stared at his piece box. Albert looked at Sean.

Did ye see that?

Aye he's a cheeky wee bastard.

The white cap looked at Sean like he was shocked. Sean gave him a wink but Albert caught him.

Ya fuckin arsehole. Ah might have guessed.

The white cap smiled and so did Sean and Albert. Sean stood up.

Ah'm goin for a fag. Are ye comin?

Albert pushed the last corner of his sandwich into his mouth and stood up. A few crumbs fell from his overalls onto the floor. Sean pointed at them.

Ya messy old bastard.

Albert gave Sean the fingers and they walked to the toilets.

Sean leaned against the washbasins and made a fag. He lit it up. Albert grabbed the lighter and lit his. He put it in his pocket. Sean put his hand out.

Cheeky bastard. Hand the lighter over.

Albert shrugged and gave it back. They had a few puffs without saying anything. Then Albert picked at a bit of tobacco hanging out of the back of his roll-up. He didn't look up as he spoke.

So where's Archie goin to stay when he gets home?

Fuck sake Albert that's six months away. How the fuck should Ah know?

It's good to get these things sorted out son. We don't want the boy goin back to crime and drugs.

Well let him stay round yours.

Ah wish Ah could but yer auntie willnay let him.

Ye wish ye could my arse. Ye don't want the cunt anywhere near ye.

Ah wouldnay say that son.

Well Ah fuckin would. Ah don't want him anywhere near me.

What about Maggie's wee sister? What's her name?

Lizzie.

Was he no seein her for a bit?

Aye but she got pregnant while he was in the jail so Ah doubt he'll be goin round there in a hurry.

But he's no had his hole for five years so —

Aye maybe. As long as he doesnay think he's stayin round mine, Ah don't gie a fuck where he goes.

Or mine.

He'll no even ask ye.

He'd be a cheeky cunt if he did.

Sean laughed.

Cheeky's his middle name but.

Albert laughed as well.

Aye Ah know.

Both of them smiled and looked at the floor. Then Albert crossed his arms over his chest.

Yer da was the same.

Was he?

Aye. Ye wouldnay believe the trouble he used to get me into.

Aye Ah would.

Albert smiled into the distance.

And yer auntie Jessie hated him.

Maggie hasnay any time for Archie.

Albert nodded.

He changed though when he met yer ma.

Pity Archie cannay settle down.

Albert looked at Sean as if he just noticed him.

What's that son?

Ah said it's a pity Archie cannay settle down.

Albert dropped his fag in the urinal.

C'mon we should get back.

Sean sat on the edge of a basin and blew some smoke rings.

Ah'll be there in a wee while.

Albert left the toilet. Sean felt good. A nice fat roll-up in the company's time.

Aye this is the life.

He swung his wellies back and forth and leaned against the mirror. Life wasn't so bad. It was just what you made it.

A pint would be nice.

The thought of the drink brought him back down. He wouldn't be having one for a while. It was going to be tight but by the time Archie was out the jail Sean should have the seven hundred saved and ready to hand over. He felt the cold mirror on the back of his head as he nodded to himself.

It fuckin better be son.

★

Albert and Jessie were goin up the toon one night so they made Archie look after me. He was fumin. Gave me a slap round the ear as soon as we were out the scheme. Just keep yer mouth shut, he said to me on the way to Sammy's. It was rainin but Ah was sweatin like a pig by the time we got there. Our Archie walks fast as fuck. Most of what Ah saw of him on the walk over was his hunched-up back, hands in his pockets, head down, and the odd gob from the side of his mouth. The only time Ah saw his face was when he turned to say c'mon hurry up ye cunt.

We got to a 74 on a peelin yellow door and Archie gave it a chap. Oh hiya Archie c'mon in said this old woman. She had a Celtic scarf over her hair and a fag in her mouth. She telt us to come in and called to Sammy yer pal's here. Archie was straight into Sammy's room tellin him Ah was there. Ah got into the room and he telt me to sit on the bed and shut it. He gave me a slap on the ear. Ah kept my mouth shut. Sammy put on a record. Same music Archie listened to at home.

Archie and Sammy sat in the corner and spoke to each other out the sides of their mouths. They looked angry and laughed and pointed fingers at each other. Ah looked around the room. Same room as ours really, same Stiff Little Fingers poster, only we had a double bed and our curtains didnay look as if someone had wiped their arse on them. Sammy asked me if Ah'd ever seen King Dong. Ah shook my head. Archie telt him to pack it in. Sammy telt him he was bein a prick. Archie said alright. He pointed at me and said but if ye tell Albert Ah'll fuckin kill ye. Ah knew he'd come close so Ah nodded. Sammy picked at one of the floorboards and pulled up a bit about a foot long.

He got on his side and put his arm all the way in and came out with a magazine. Ah couldnay believe it. There was a black guy with a cock that went down past his knees. Sammy said King Dong fainted every time he got a hard on. Ah bet ye his wife does as well said Archie. They laughed and Sammy took the magazine back and put it under the floor. Sammy pulled somethin else out and telt me to watch the bedroom door. Ah could hardly hear them for the music but the polis were mentioned.

On the way home Archie gave me fifty pence for sweeties and telt me Ah'd seen fuck-all, right?

A few nights later we were sat in the house and Archie seemed a bit jumpy. Every time a motor drove onto the street he got up and looked out the window. My auntie Jessie asked him if he had ants in his pants. My uncle Albert looked up, growled at Archie and got back to the paper. Ah watched the telly. Then Archie got really agitated and there was a knock at the door. My uncle got up to get it and came into the livin room with these two polis. He telt me to get to my bed. He telt Archie to get sat on his arse.

Ah heard a bit of shoutin downstairs then Archie came up. Ah asked him what was goin on. He telt me to mind my own business and gave me a punch on the top of my head. It was fuckin sore. Ah ran downstairs greetin just as my uncle was showin the polis out the front door. Ah went into the livin room and my auntie Jessie gave me a cuddle. My uncle shut the door and went upstairs. Ah heard him gie Archie a batterin. By the time Ah went back up he seemed to be asleep but when Ah got into bed he grabbed me by the hair and telt me he'd fuckin kill me if Ah ever grassed him up again. It was that sore Ah nearly pished myself.

*

Sean finished his fag and walked down the corridor and back into Fresh. He looked over at the women but they were all busy and didn't notice him passing. He couldn't be bothered giving them a shout. One of the older women was showing a new lassie how to truss up a chicken. She was laughing because she couldn't get the elastic round the chicken's legs. The old one showed her three times before she finally managed it on her own. She looked best-pleased when she done it and the old dear winked at her and said that's my girl. Sean spat on the floor and climbed the steps to his station.

He heard the psst-psst-psst and had to run. The birds being pumped onto his conveyor were plump ones. Sunday roasters. Lovely when they're cooked. A light brown skin, toes turned up, and a waft of aromatic steam tempting the taste buds. The dad at the head of the table, sharpening the carving knife with long deliberate flicks. The children hypnotised by the rhythmic scrapes yet alert as hungry dogs. The sprouts and the mash potatoes are on dishes in the centre of the table. They're dying to nick a sprout but any funny business and the dad will delay the serving of the chicken for another few minutes. A lesson in self-discipline he calls it. Mum comes through from the kitchen with the roasting can smoking with potatoes and vegetables. She pours the contents of the can into a warmed dish placed in the centre of the table and goes back for the Yorkshire puds. In and out the dining room she is, head pecking the air like a busy busy chicken, placing random condiments on the table, until she hangs her pinafore on the back of the kitchen door and fetches through the gravy. She places it on a mat, souvenir of Minehead North Devon 1985, and waits patiently for the husband to serve up the meat. He cuts into the brown breast to reveal the pure white meat below and places a slice on his wife's plate. Thanks darling she says. He serves up portions of the chicken to all the family leaving himself till last. Of course he saved himself a nice thick bit of breast, he is the breadwinner after all. Mum tells the children to help themselves to vegetables and they do. She picks out two choice roast potatoes and a Yorkshire pudding for her husband. A bit of roast parsnip, a spoonful of creamy mash, some sprouts and carrots and the dinner is ready for a liberal splash of home-made gravy. Mum does this for the whole family. She holds a tea towel against the edge of the gravy boat to make sure none drips on the embroidered tablecloth given to her and her husband as a wedding present. He is cutting into the flesh with a knife, fork poised above the repast, when he notices a piece of paper jutting from the chicken's arse. What's this? he says to his wife. I don't know darling, why don't you have a look? He reads the note out and his wife drops her cutlery and spits her barely chewed first mouthful onto her plate. Can she taste the spunk of a factory hand? Nice.

Sean sniggered at the thought of the fortune chickens he has sent into the world of the happy family. The most important thing was not to do it very often. Once in a blue moon and he'd never get caught. He'd deny it anyway. Prove it he'd say.

Prove what? said Albert.

What are ye doin over here?

Never mind that, what are ye goin on about?

Nothing, Ah was just talkin to myself.

Oh aye? It'll be hairs on the palms of the hands next.

Tell me about it, this place drives me fuckin nuts. Them cunts should be offerin us counsellin or somethin.

Counsellin?

Aye. What's funny about that?

Albert walked back to his station shaking his head and muttering counselling.

Sean struggled on with the Sunday roasters. A half-hour's aerobic workout with them leaves the forearms zinging. You don't just pick them up. You have to get your elbows under your wrists and swing them in the direction of the conveyor. Otherwise your wrists take the strain and before you know it you've lifted your last pint. That would be a tragedy. And Sean is not having that. When he retires he wants to be able to pick up a pint without wincing. These big ones don't half pull but. Thank god they're not like that all day. You'd end up crippled.

A chicken landed on the conveyor, its legs spread like

a woman that's just dropped a baby, gaping minge telling him he's a man and thank fuck for that. Sean wondered if Maggie was up and about yet. It must be half eight. She might be walking down the Royston Road with Donna. Long dark hair and blokes looking at them, seeing the mother and the potential in the daughter. One of them van drivers slowing down as he passes so he can have a look at their faces. The thing with Maggie is she's got a delicious wee arse. Like two peaches it is. Any man can be forgiven for having a look. She just smiles though. Not one of them tarty smiles. The smile of a woman who appreciates the compliment but is happy with the man she's got, thank you very much. She might even nod when he winks at her but she won't wink back.

Of course she'll get to the school and one of the teachers will come out to meet her. No doubt that Mr Keyes. Sean remembered him at the parents' night. All sugar to the women. The trouble with teachers like that is they've had too much time with kids doing what they're told. It gives them the idea they're a bit of a character. Bit of a geezer. Lapping up the attentions of giggling lassies. Maggie wasn't impressed either. Did you see the dog hair on his jacket? she said when they were walking home.

A chicken dropped and bounced to the side of the conveyor belt. Sean grabbed it by the thigh and tugged. It got wedged between the belt and the framework and he had to yank it free. It felt like it didn't want to leave the conveyor belt. Didn't want to be clicked onto hooks to disappear and be trussed and wrapped ready for the

sticker with the bar code and the price and the fluorescent display on the supermarket shelf.

Sean could see Maggie pushing the trolley round the
shop. The vegetables first, potatoes and carrots and that,
placed on the bottom. Then a layer of fruit. Tangerines,
oranges, apples and bananas. Then she goes to the meat
counter. Sausages, mince, and a chat with the butcher.
Her smile and eyes and Royston-bred sharpness get a
piece of steak as tender as a mother with a bleeding child.

The butcher shows her a special offer on chicken
breasts. But she tells him her husband gets them at his
work. She pushes the trolley towards the bread. Bum
tensing with the weight. The shop manager having a
look and his eyebrows going up. Maggie notices him
noticing her. She smiles. He smiles. Do you need any
help? he says to her. No thanks she says I come here
every week and know what I want. OK he says but if
you need anything give me a shout. He winks at her.

Maggie goes to the bakery section and picks over
loaves till she finds one with the most distant sell-by
date. She does the same with the milk. She gets some
juice for Donna, a packet of chocolate biscuits and half
a dozen cans of lager. She gets herself ten Mayfair to
see her alright until Sean comes back from work.

When she's finished she takes her purchases to the
fat woman on the checkout. As the shopping is beeped
through the till they talk about the price of butter. The
woman asks her if she heard about the pensioner who
got mugged on Wednesday. Maggie shakes her head.
Right outside her front door says the woman. Terrible
Maggie says, probably drugs.

Maggie pays and struggles out of the supermarket with four bags of shopping. She puts them down at the taxi rank. While she's waiting a youth asks her for some change for a cup of tea. She looks at the boy and reaches for her purse. She gives him fifty pence and tells him not to spend it on drink. She puts her purse back and gets out her fags. She shakes her hair out of the way of the flame as she lights it and takes a long drag. She blows the smoke towards the sky, her gold necklace glinting in the winter sun.

CHAPTER 4

George appeared with two white caps.

Are ye busy?

Sean turned from his station.

It's no been too bad the day.

George nodded.

Ye can drive can ye no?

Aye. Ah passed my test a coupla years ago.

Good. Ah've a wee job for ye.

Sean pointed to his station.

What about this?

George nodded at the white caps.

That's what these two are for. As long as the line isnay too busy they'll be alright.

Well it isnay.

They'll be a few less comin through anyway.

How, what's up?

We've got a bit of an emergency.

George turned to the white caps.

Right yous two, take over here.

He shouted across the Junction.

Albert.

Aye.

George walked towards the exit.

Follow me.

Sean and Albert looked at each other and shrugged their shoulders. As much as they didn't like being ordered about, it was always a relief to get called away from the line.

They followed George through Fresh and out into the corridor. When they got near the offices he turned round to Sean.

Ah've got a wee message Ah want yous to run. D'ye know the way to Falkirk?

Aye.

Good. We've been delivered the wrong size of shrink-wrap and they cannay get any more to us before Monday. Overstretched they said, the lazy bastards. So anyway, Ah thought Ah'd gie yous the pleasure of a wee run out to pick up the right stuff.

Sean found it hard to stop smiling. He nudged Albert in the ribs.

Fuckin brilliant eh? Ah've no been to Falkirk for years.

Albert looked miserable.

Magic.

George gave Albert a funny look and went into the office. He came back out with a clipboard under his arm and a set of keys in his hand.

Here ye are.

Sean grabbed the keys and put them in his jacket pocket.

They walked out of the rear of the factory and onto a diesel-stained yard. Two lorries were parked with their backs in the loading bay. Forklifts were running in and out with pallets of chickens. The lorry drivers were having a fag and a chat. George nodded at the lorries.

We've got a lot of birds to be delivered over the weekend.

Sean noticed the we.

Aye.

George frowned.

And we'll be runnin out of wrap by this afternoon. Ye cannay send chickens to Tesco's without a package.

Sean tried to laugh.

Aye they wouldnay have that.

They crossed the concrete yard to the garage. George pulled the little door open and they stepped through. It looked like the door in a prison. At the back there was a chain system that George pulled and the main doors opened. Light shone through the garage and onto a white transit van with rust stains around the head-lights. Albert pointed at it.

We're no goin in that old banger are we?

That's all there is. The other vans are out on deliv-eries. If there was any of them there Ah'd get the driver to do this job. But it's Friday and —

Ye have to scrape the barrel.

George nodded as he echoed Albert's words.

Barrel.

Sean went over to the van and climbed into the driver's seat. He turned the keys until the glow light went off then he clicked on the starter. The engine barked a few times before it roared into life. He drove the van to the entrance of the garage and climbed out. He left it running to warm it up. It had the odd beat of an old engine. He wondered if it would make it to Falkirk and back.

Sean leaned on the van's front wing and kicked the tyre. Albert crossed his hands over his chest. George got his clipboard out. Black smoke drifted round from the back of the van and started Albert coughing.

Jesus fuckin Christ he said between gasps.

Sean banged him on the back and Albert coughed till there was saliva running down his chin. He wiped his mouth.

That thing's fucked.

George rested his hand on the van.

She'll be alright.

He showed Sean the clipboard. They stood side by side while George went through the bits of paper.

This is the original order form. Ah've circled the goods they got wrong.

Sean nodded and George turned over the page.

And this is the invoice. See the difference?

Aye.

Anyway Ah've phoned them so they should know but ye can explain it yerself if it's an awkward cunt on the loadin bay.

Aye.

And if they gie ye too much shite just tell them to phone me.

Sean nodded and George patted him on the back.

Good man.

Albert looked at George.

So how come ye need the two of us?

Ye'll need to load the van up. There might be no fucker at the other end and the rolls are too heavy for one guy to lift.

Albert nodded.

Fair enough.

George gave Sean the clipboard.

Right then boys.

He looked at his watch.

Ah'll see yous in an hour or so.

George nodded.

Oh and boys?

Aye.

He pointed at a scaffold bar leaning against the wall of the garage.

Put that in the van. Ye'll need it to lift the rolls.

Sean picked one end of the bar up and dragged it to the back of the van. The door opened with a creak. He slid the bar onto the back ledge and punted it inside. It bounced off the driver's seat and left a big gouge in it. He walked round to the front of the van and Albert sniggered.

Temper temper.

Good enough for the cunts.

They climbed into the van and slammed the doors shut. Sean let the clutch out and they shuddered forward. Albert held his hat on his head.

Ah thought ye could drive?

Sean put the van into second and it lurched again.

Ah'm no used to the clutch.

Fuckin prick.

Aye Ah know ye are.

Albert held on to the door handle.

Just take it easy. If ye crash this rust bucket the two of us are fucked.

Sean felt barely in control of the van as it slewed towards the factory gates. The security guard saw them coming and got the barrier up just in time. They flew past him, Sean struggling with the steering wheel and Albert trying to find his seat belt.

The T-junction at the end of the drive came up really quick and Sean put the brakes on. They weren't very good so he stomped on them and the van skidded to a halt about a foot into the road. A lorry went past with its horn blaring. Albert bounced against the dashboard and back before he managed to get the seat belt attached.

For fuck sake. Are ye tryin to get us killed?

Sean fell back into his seat and watched their breath steam up the windows. He tried to turn the fan on but it didn't work.

This van's fucked.

Ah telt ye that in the yard.

He found a rag in the driver's door and cleaned the condensation off the windows. He reached for the indicators and turned the windscreen wipers on. Albert muttered something. Sean poked about the steering column till he found the indicators and signalled left. He revved the engine and slowly let out the clutch. The van moved into the road and Sean went up through the gears. He could feel the vibrations coming through the steering wheel and the gearstick but the van didn't lurch about so much if he was gentle with the controls.

Albert nodded.

That's more like it.

Sean felt pleased.

It's fuckin noisy eh?

Aye. It should've been pensioned off years ago.

What, like yerself?

Cheeky wee cunt.

They got to the dual-carriageway without any incidents and Sean put his foot down a bit until they merged with the other traffic. He looked in the mirror. A spiral of exhaust smoke disappeared into the distance.

Make us a fag uncle.

Albert pulled his tobacco out, made a couple of fags and passed a lit one to his nephew. Sean had a couple of deep draws.

This is the fuckin life.

Albert put his wellies up on the dashboard.

Beats workin on a fuckin line. Ah'll tell ye that for nothin.

Sean pulled himself up by the steering wheel.

But ye were actin all sulky when George asked us to do this.

Fuckin right Ah was.

How come?

Albert took a draw on his fag and flicked the ash on the floor.

Ah wanted to make sure the cunt knew we were doin him a favour.

Sean felt like a bit of a prick.

Oh aye.

Albert laughed and touched the side of his nose.

Aye ye've got a lot to learn wee man. But stick with yer old uncle and ye'll go a long way.

D'ye think so?

Aye. Coz ye've a long way to go.

Ha fuckin ha.

The van slowed as they climbed the hill next to Cumbernauld. Cars went past them. Even a lorry went past them. Sean held the steering wheel tight to stop the van being buffeted into the grass verge. He put the wipers on as fast as they would go to clear the spray from the windscreen. Albert pointed up to Cumbernauld.

Me and yer auntie Jessie nearly moved there.

How come?

They were knockin down the tenements and scatterin us all over the place. We had a choice. Easterhouse –

Fuck that.

Or Royston or here.

Sean checked out the countryside and nodded his head.

It looks alright here.

Aye maybe. But yer auntie wasnay so sure. When ye cannay drive it's a fair distance from the family so we thought fuck it, and stayed in the toon.

Aye Royston's alright. And this place looks as if it might be a bit quiet.

Ye can say that again. It was even worse back then coz they didnay have any pubs in the place.

Yer kiddin.

No, Ah'm serious.

Sean didn't know whether to believe him or not.

At the top of the hill the road curved away into the distance and under the railway arches at Castlecary. Sean pointed ahead.

Some view eh?

Albert cracked open his window to let out the smoke.

Aye it sure is. Them Victorians knew how to build railways. Ah bet ye it was some site in the old days. The old mail train would puff along there behind a big head of steam. Ye could see them comin for miles.

Sean went to ask him more about the steam trains but he noticed the old boy was gazing out the window. Sean focused through the windscreen and sighed. He pressed the throttle to the floor and felt the van vibrate as the speed built up.

★

Albert and Jessie had to go to a funeral in Ireland. Some cousin of Jessie's. They were goin to be away for three days. Albert had a quiet word with Archie. Ah'm trustin ye now son. If anythin happens while Ah'm away. Anythin to the house or yer wee brother and Ah'll be holdin ye responsible. They'll be consequences. That's no a threat son, that's a promise. Archie was too busy plannin what he'd do with the freedom. He wasnay payin attention. He wished he had though. Ah can tell ye that.

They left on the Monday mornin and straight away Archie was on the phone to Sammy. Said he could stay with us for a coupla days. That he could sleep in the double with me and Archie would sleep in Albert and

Jessie's bed. Last thing Ah wanted was to be sleepin with Sammy but it was either that or the couch.

Monday night was pandemonium. We came back from school and Ah had to make them a fry for their dinner. Ah did my best but the eggs were a bit crispy and the toast was burnt on one side. They put about half a bottle of tomato sauce on theirs and ate it with their elbows out and plenty of rifts. Then it was the feet up on the kitchen table and a fag each while Ah washed the dishes. Archie said Ah'd make somebody a good wife and Sammy sniggered. They went out and left me in the house. Ah was watchin *Coronation Street* when the phone went. It was my auntie Jessie. Was everythin alright? Ah said aye, that we'd had our tea and was doin my homework. Put Archie on the phone she said. Ah telt her he'd gone out with Sammy and the phone went a bit quiet. Then my uncle Albert came on. Where is he? Ah don't know. Tell him if that Sammy McCann comes into my house Ah'll fuckin kill the pair of them. OK. Ah put the phone down.

Archie and Sammy came in at nine. They were stinkin of glue. Archie had loads of it stuck round his face. Sammy sat in the chair and stared at me. Ah got up and he asked me to make him a cup of tea doll. Ah telt him to fuck off and ran up the stairs. Archie shouted at me. Don't talk to my pals like that ya cunt. Ah slammed the bedroom door and lay on the bed. Ah thought he'd follow me up and gie me a slap but he never. A little while later Ah heard the front door go and Ah hoped they were out till mornin. But Ah felt Sammy get into bed with me durin the night.

The next mornin Archie gave me a pound for my dinner money. Ah was chuffed coz school dinners only cost twelve and a half pee. As Ah was goin out the front door Ah could hear him tellin Sammy to get downstairs and get the fuckin kettle on. Ah was glad to be out. Last thing Ah wanted was to be their slave all day. They'd probably make me tie a tea towel into the front of my trousers so Ah looked like a waiter.

The house stunk of feet and sweat when Ah got back. It's rotten in here Ah said and Sammy called me a cheeky wee cunt and wriggled his big toe through a hole in his sock. Him and Archie were playin brag on the kitchen table. They had a pile of pound notes between them. Archie looked at the clock on the kitchen wall and said come on Sammy we better move. He scooped up the money and gave me a pound. He telt me it was my wages for washin up and Ah should get some chips for my tea. Ah asked where they were goin. To see a man about a dug he said and touched the side of his nose. He said they might have a wee treat for me later. If Jessie phoned Ah was to tell her they were at the youth club.

Ah was just settlin down with a quarter of Kola Kubes, a bottle of Irn Bru and *World in Action* when Sammy put his head round the door and telt me to help bring in a bag of coal. Ah pulled on my trainers and my jacket and walked into the road. Archie was sittin in the drivin seat of an Escort Mexico revvin the engine. C'mon to fuck Sean we've no got all day he shouted and flicked a fag-end into the road. Sammy held the door open and Ah climbed in the back. As

Sammy was gettin in Archie let the clutch go and we wheel-spinned up the street. Sammy fell into the seat goin for fuck sake. Archie laughed and my head hit the window as the motor flew sideways round the corner and into the main road. Jackie Stewart eat yer fuckin heart out he shouted and Ah didnay know whether to laugh or be sick.

The first thing we did was a fill-up and fuck-off at the petrol station in Kilsyth. Lesson number one Archie called it. Ye cannay run out of juice when the polis are on yer tail. We headed towards Falkirk. Good drivin roads Archie said. And maybe a wee country house with some trinkets for the boys. Sammy said he knew just the place and telt Archie to take the next right. And slow the fuck down, ye can hear the motor all the way to Edinburgh. We turned into a single-track lane and Archie turned the lights off. Lesson number two, surprise is our biggest weapon he said and turned round to look at me. Sammy said he'd been readin too many *Commando* comics. He drove for a few hundred yards and let the car glide to a stop outside a house. Sammy got out and went to the door. He gave it a good knock. Nobody answered. He waved and Archie pulled a pair of socks out of his pocket and telt me to wait in the car. Ah saw him pull the socks over his hands as he approached the house.

It was scary waitin in the car. Ah heard a window breakin and things crashin and every time a car passed on the main road Ah thought it was the polis. Eventually Archie and Sammy appeared from the side of the house carryin a bed sheet between them. They ran to the back of the car and Ah felt the suspension go down with the weight of it. The boot slammed and they were in the car. They were gigglin like wee lassies. Archie drove with no lights till we got on the main road. Then he was off like Jackie Stewart again.

We went to a scheme in Falkirk and knocked on a door. A guy with a borstal dot answered. When he saw the bed sheet hangin between Archie and Sammy he looked up and down the street and telt us to come in. Who's the wee fella? he said. His gold rings nipped my fingers when he shook my hand. He pointed to a bedroom and telt Archie to put that in there. Me and Sammy went into the livin room. Everybody was smokin and drinkin and talkin. Ah couldnay understand them coz of their accents. Ah stood in the corner and watched Sammy. He swigged out of a bottle of Irn Bru and pointed it at me. There wasnay much left so Ah said no.

We got twenty bar and a quarter of red leb for the stuff. Sammy made a joint and we drove down the main street with the radio blarin. We saw a copper and Sammy was goin no c'mon to fuck let's get out of here. But Archie slowed the motor and rolled his window down. Excuse me mate he said. The polis came over to the window and bent down to look in. Archie spat on him and wheel-spinned away. Ah turned and saw the polis with his radio to his ear and his other hand rubbin his uniform with a hanky. Sammy was ragin. We'll get a batterin if they catch us now he said. Archie laughed. Where's yer sense of humour ya cunt? he said. Sammy looked out the window. Ah said nothin.

Archie pushed the throttle down and we roared out

of the toon. Fuckin shitehole we called it and gave the fingers to the Welcome to Falkirk Please Drive Carefully sign. We were comin into the country and Archie looked in the mirror. Don't look behind ye Sean but the polis are up my arse. Ah couldnay resist a look but. There were two of them in an Austin Allegro. They drew quite close and Ah could see the passenger talkin on the radio. Sammy was tellin Archie how he knew this was goin to happen and he hoped Archie was satisfied with himself. Archie telt him to shut the fuck up. He kept at an even thirty. Ah gave the police motor the fingers. Their blue lights started flashin. Archie dropped a gear and we were off like Jackie Stewart.

The swervin motor knocked me flat on the back seat. All Ah could see was flashin lights and Sammy's face as he tried to look out the back window. Then the car braked and Ah ended up on the floor. Ah nearly shat myself lyin there listenin to the tyres screech as we flew round corners. They're still there the cunts said Archie. Sammy said put yer foot down for fuck sake. She'll no go any faster said Archie. Ah could feel him push the front seat back as he squeezed on the throttle. He slowed the car down and said we'll never get away from the cunts this way. Ah climbed back onto the back seat and saw him pass Sammy a beer tin. Sammy said what are ye doin? Shut up and do what yer telt. Sammy leaned out of the window and threw the beer tin straight through the coppers' windscreen. Easy-fuckin-peasy said Archie as we drove off.

We thought it would be best to head towards Glesga. No the way we came though. Over the hills and through the Carron valley. There's never any polis up there. It's like the Highlands said Sammy, single-track roads and people leavin their doors open at night. Archie's eyes lit up at the thought of all them unlocked houses, but Sammy said we should try and get home before we get captured. Archie called him a big fuckin shitebag.

We stopped at one of them tourist viewpoints near the top of the hill. Sammy skinned another joint. They gave me a coupla puffs. No too much though, we cannay have the wee cunt spewin in the motor said Archie. When it was finished we sat quiet for a while. Ye could see the gas flares of Grangemouth on one side and the lights in the Glesga flats on the other. Then Archie made a fartin sound and we all burst out laughin.

He started the motor up and we had an easy drive along country roads goin in and out of pine forests. We thought about callin in to the Carron Bridge Hotel but there was a polis motor in the car park so we drove past. Somethin had gave the game away but coz the cunt was straight out after us. It was a Cortina. We wouldnay get away from that so easy. Archie tried his best. Ah hung on to the back of his seat. Sammy had his feet up against the dashboard. Every time we hit a corner Ah thought we were off into the blue flashin trees.

Then we came to a long straight bit up the side of the loch. Archie took the car up to seventy. He braked for an S-bend. The motor spun comin out the first corner. It was too much for him and we went into the second at the wrong angle. We hit the side of the road and the car went up, through a fence, hung in the air, then bang, fuck ye, right into a tree.

Ah came to in the hospital with my auntie Jessie holdin my hand goin he's awake, he's awake, my wee boy's awake. Tears were runnin down her cheeks. Oh son what have they done to ye? My leg was broken in three places, Ah had cracked ribs and my collarbone was fractured. Archie was at the foot of the bed lookin sheepish. His face was covered in bruises and there was a buckle mark on his neck. My uncle Albert shook his head at my plastered leg. He turned round and growled at Archie. Ah telt ye they'd be consequences ya cunt. Archie said nothin.

Sammy and Archie got six months each in Glenochil. It turned out they'd been stealin cars for months. They'd screwed half a dozen houses on the scheme. They'd even broken into the post office and one of the dirty bastards had done a shite in the till. My auntie Jessie was mortified. She reckoned she could feel the neighbours starin at her every time she went to the shop. Talkin about them O'Gradys so they were.

Archie always said Glenochil made a man of him. Ye had to fight for everythin includin yer own body. Sammy was quiet when he came out. He wasnay as good a fighter as Archie. Ah was lucky. All Ah got was a warnin from the sheriff.

★

They turned off the dual-carriageway and before long they passed the Welcome to Falkirk sign. The traffic lights turned red and Sean braked. Albert snorted when

the slowing van jerked him out of his half sleep. It was
pretty busy but then it was nine in the morning. They
pulled away from the lights and along a tree-lined street
that had glimpses of big houses in the background.

Ah wouldnay mind stayin here.

Ah wouldnay mind the money it cost to stay here.
The van stuttered into the town. They stopped at a set
of lights and it stalled. It took a few turns of the starter
before it came back to life. By that time people were
peeping their horns. Sean gave them the fingers and
nearly stalled the van again as he drove away.

Fuckin heap of shite.

Ah telt ye.
They eventually made it through the town centre. Albert
pointed at a sign for the industrial estate.

That's it there.

Ah know.

Ah'm just sayin.
They pulled up at red and black barrier stretched across
a gap in a barbed wire fence. Sean gave the horn a peep.
An old guy came out of a hut and lifted up the barrier.
Sean drove the van into the yard and reversed it up to
the loading bay.

A man in a white coat came out and looked at the
chitty.

Aye they're always fuckin these orders up.
White coat nodded to a door and walked through it.

C'mon then.
Albert and Sean got out the van and went into the
bay. They followed the guy through the door and saw
the delivery. Rolls and rolls of shrink-wrap piled

against a wall. The guy in the white coat pointed at them.

There ye go. That's yer order there. Gie's a shout when yer ready.

Where are ye goin?

Ah've got work to do.

Are ye no helpin us to load it?

White coat laughed.

Am Ah fuck.

What about a cup of tea then?

Ah'll send one out in a wee while.

Sean and Albert looked at each other. Then Sean opened the van up and pulled the scaffold bar out the back. He put it through the middle of a roll of wrap and Albert grabbed the other end. They lifted the roll into the van. Sean went in first because that is the hardest part and Albert's old. He banged his head on the roof of the van.

Ya fuckin bastard. This is awkward as fuck.

It only took them ten minutes to load up the rolls of wrap. Then white coat appeared with the cups of tea.

Milk and two sugars?

Magic.

They took the cups and sat on the back step of the van. A fag each and they were well relaxed. The tea was hot. The steam off it made Sean's nose run. He sniffed and pulled up a mouthful of snot and spat it in the yard. Albert grimaced.

That's fuckin charmin.

Sean laughed and wiped his nose with his sleeve.

Sorry.

Sean held his cup with his two hands. The heat was lovely. He nudged Albert.

Remember the last time Ah was in Falkirk?

Albert laughed.

Ya pair of wee bastards.

Ah, we were only boys.

At least one of ye grew out of that carry on.

Sean nodded and stood up.

Aye Ah know.

He reached for Albert's mug.

Are ye finished?

Albert took a last swig and gave Sean the mug. Sean walked into the loading bay.

There's yer mugs he shouted.

White coat came out and took them.

Hang on.

He went back in and appeared with another chitty.

Sign this.

Sean signed and white coat tore him the top copy.

Cheers pal.

The van started first time and they drove out of the yard. It was best to go a bit slower because it jumped about on the corners with all the weight in the back.

Ah'll take it easy on the way back.

Albert put his feet back on the dashboard and pulled his cap down over his eyes.

Good idea son.

Sean shook his head and smiled.

And Ah'll go and see Sammy as soon as we get there.

Albert mumbled something Sean couldn't hear.

Chapter 5

It was alright at home while Archie was in Glenochil coz Ah had a bed to myself for a while. The first thing Ah done was ask my uncle if Gambo could come round for his dinner and stay the night. My auntie Jessie put on a bit of a spread. There was pieces on corned beef, ham and cheese. Irn Bru and crisps and they wee sausages ye get at parties. And some pickled onions. Gambo couldnay believe his luck. His da was a bit of a waster so they didnay get luxuries like that in their house.

Between stuffin his gub and swallowin he didnay have much breath for talkin but he managed that as well. My auntie Jessie was impressed with what he had to say. She thought he was a clever wee laddie and Ah should take a leaf out of his book.

Then he telt them about the bible classes. My uncle Albert nearly sprayed his dinner on the table. He kept nudgin me and noddin at Gambo as if he was some sort of idiot. He telt us the churches were only interested in how much money they could screw out of the poor. But my auntie was impressed. She couldnay see anythin wrong with youngsters takin an interest in the bible. And anyway we shouldnay be sniggerin at the poor boy's beliefs. My uncle shut up at that. But every time he looked out the window Ah knew he was tryin no to laugh.

Then Gambo got onto the trip the bible class was organisin. The train down to Ayr to stay in an old country house for a week. My uncle said it sounded pretty grand and it would be nice for me to go. But no doubt it would cost a fuckin packet so never mind son. He gied me his tight-lipped smile. Then Gambo played his ace. But the trip only costs two pound Mr O'Grady, the bible class are stumpin up the other tenner.

That would be good for the boy. Broaden his horizons said my auntie. My uncle looked at her. Aye it would he said. But they'd only fill his head with that Christian shite. He'd come back thinkin he was a martyr for the cause and we'd get tutted every time we swore. Ah shook my head and promised Ah wouldnay let them brainwash me. Albert nodded and telt Gambo to get an application.

On the day of the trip we all had to meet down Central Station. Ah saw my uncle talkin to one of the leaders from the bible class. The guy looked a bit red in the face and Ah hoped he wasnay gettin threatened. Then the whistle blew and we climbed onto the train. A last wave to the relatives and we were off.

The scenery was nice on the way. Green fields and sheep and cows. The leaders got us to sing songs and play stupid card games. One of them telt us that every time we flushed the toilet it ended up on the track.

When we got to Ayr it was a minibus that took us up to the country house. That was where my trouble started. Some guy behind us in a flash motor gied me a wave. Ah gied him the fingers. Gambo was eggin me on so Ah kept it up. Eventually the guy managed to overtake but the rotten old bastard stopped the van and telt one of the leaders. The leader was well embarrassed. He pulled me aside when we got to the house. Telt me he'd saw my sort before and if Ah gied him any bother Ah'd get a hard kick up the arse. And if that wasnay enough to warn me, there would be no puddin after my dinner.

The next day they gied us a map each and a push-bike and telt us to meet up in some cafe in the toon. It was alright coz Ah jumped in there quick and didnay get lumbered with a lassie's bike. Or a shopper. Me and Gambo managed to get teamed up the gether so we went for a wander in the country. We found a stream and it was that warm we thought we'd have a swim. There was clegs everywhere and Ah got bit to fuck but it was worth it. Before we left we had a shite in the water and watched them float away downstream. Mine was a bit lighter than Gambo's. Probably coz Ah'd missed out on the chocolate puddin.

The toon was a quiet wee place. The first shop we went into had one old woman workin in it. Gambo asked her if he could look at a tartan doll on a shelf behind the counter. As soon as her back was turned Ah grabbed a coupla ornaments. One of them was this wee brass cannon with a coat of arms on it and Ayrshire in fancy writin. My auntie was well pleased and telt me Ah should have spent my money on myself. Ah gied the other one to Gambo for his ma. He said she put it straight on the mantelpiece and telt all the neighbours it was a present from her boy.

We got to the cafe about an hour after everybody else and the leader gied me a load more shite. Said Ah was thick as well as cheeky. Ah thought fuck him coz Ah knew Ah wasnay goin to spend my life leadin a bunch of weans round the country. And it didnay get much better. Ah accidentally threw a snooker ball through the livin room window that night so Ah didnay get any puddin again.

Then after dinner they gathered us all into a room and telt us about the path to Christ. It was a long hard road with cunts giein ye grief and that. But it was worth it in the end when ye were relaxin in the arms of baby Jesus. The road to hell was easy. Just like a motorway and as fast. Satan would help ye get through this life but when it came to the big sleep ye were in for an eternity of hellfire and hot pokers up the arse. The leaders even made it more realistic with a picture of a mountain with a tight wee path on it and a cliff with a big fire at the bottom.

Ah was half convinced so Ah asked the leader how did Ah take the path to Jesus. His eyes lit up and he said he was sorry he was hard on me but it was coz he knew Ah had the potential to hold the spirit of the lord. But Ah had a strong will that needed to be broke for my own good. Ah believed the cunt. He telt me to ask Jesus to come into my heart when Ah was in bed that night.

On the way back to the dorm Gambo could hardy walk for laughin. He pointed at me and called me a teacher's pet and a fuckin idiot. The only thing God was good for was Christmas. And even that wasnay all that good. We got into our beds and Ah waited till the lights went out and Gambo had stopped sniggerin.

Please Jesus, Ah said, come into my heart and save me from evil. Ah could hear a wee whisper and for a minute Ah thought Ah was saved. But it was Gambo. The cunt burst out laughin and telt me Ah was a fuckin poof and wait till we got home and he telt everybody about it. Ah telt him to shut his fuckin mouth and we ended up havin a fight. A leader appeared and split us up. Ah telt him Gambo was takin the piss out of me and the leader went daft. Gambo never got any puddin the next night.

Ah hated fallin out with Gambo. He spent the rest of the holiday knockin about with some guy from Paisley. The two of them made suckin noises every time they passed me in the corridor.

Ah was a Christian till the train got halfway back to the toon. The magic started to wear off by then. Ah looked at Gambo and he would tut and look out of the window. Ah went and sat next to him anyway. Ah offered him a sweetie Ah'd saved from the shops in Ayr. He took it and Ah telt him Ah was sorry for bein a Christian. He said he was sorry for takin the piss out of me. Ah telt him Ah would pack in the bible thumpin if he would promise no to tell anybody about it. Especially my uncle or Archie. Gambo clattered the sweetie round his mouth and promised.

★

Sean drove into the yard at the back of the factory. He gave the horn a long peep. Albert snorted.

What? Ah'll be there in a minute.

He looked at Sean and smiled. His fist came to his mouth as he yawned. Then he stretched and scraped his fingers along the roof of the van.

Back in one piece then?

Ha fuckin ha. Had a good sleep?

Albert smacked his lips.

Aye lovely.

George came out and waved.

My saviours have returned.

Sean rolled the window down.

Where d'ye want them rolls?

George smiled.

Never mind them. Yous two take yerselves down the canteen for a cup of tea.

He looked at his watch.

Have another ten minutes then send the white caps to see me.

George disappeared back into the factory. Albert looked at Sean and winked.

Telt ye.

Sean clicked the lock on his door and climbed out. He cracked his knuckles and had a wee stretch as he walked to the entrance. George came back out with a couple of men. He told them to take the wrap down to Packing.

Sean walked up to George.

Can Ah have a word?

George turned to Sean.

Aye pal.

Ah've got a wee bit of business to sort out. Is it alright if Ah do it now?

George turned to Albert.

Have yer tea Albert and send one of the boys back when yer finished. Leave the other one till Sean gets back.

Cheers George. Yer a star.

No bother son. One good turn deserves another.

The paperwork's in the van.

Alright. Away and get yer tea.

George turned to the men.

Right come on boys get that van unloaded.

Albert and Sean walked into the factory. They got to the corridor next to Fresh and Albert went to the canteen. He called over his shoulder.

Mind in get me two pouches of Golden Virginia.

Aye alright.

Sean swaggered down the corridor and pushed through the doors into Fresh. He walked down the side of a conveyor belt and said hello to the women as he passed them. They trussed chickens with the casualness of grannies putting on nappies. Sean half expected to see a cloud of baby powder or to hear one of them making pigeon sounds while she tickled a chicken's breast. But he never, all he saw was chicken after chicken having its legs tied up and laid on a polystyrene tray on a conveyor belt. Head first they disappeared into a machine that wrapped them in cling film. Then they were weighed and labelled with a price and an idea for a recipe from the South of France or India or Mexico.

Crates and crates of them were stacked on pallets and dragged by human donkeys to Rab, who loaded them onto refrigerated trucks.

When Sean got to the edge of Fresh and into Packing he caught sight of Rab disappearing into his hut. Sean walked over and looked inside. Rab had his feet on a desk and was flicking through a magazine.

Alright wee man?

Rab took his feet off the desk.

Alright pal?

Sean leaned against the door jamb of the shed.

Aye magic. What are ye up to?

Nothin but load chickens.

Sean nodded at the magazine.

Aye and what else?

It's my only vice.

Aye apart from beer, hash and fags.

Rab opened the magazine to the centre spread.

But look at this thing.

She's no bad. Nice tits.

Check out the Cornish pasty.

Sean nodded like a wine connoisseur.

Lovely.

Rab's eyes sparkled.

Imagine havin a bird like that. Ye'd never come to work.

Ye'd have to come to work to be able to afford it.

No. Ye could live off her earnins.

Ah suppose yer right.

Sean pushed himself off the door jamb.

Anyway, have ye seen Sammy?

Rab pointed a thumb over his shoulder.

He's in Frozen.

Sean left Packing and took the short cut through Portions. It was mainly men worked in here. Men with sharp knives and chain-mail gloves grabbed chickens and cut them into individual portions. You go into the supermarket and you think how considerate, they have chopped a chicken into portions. How much easier is this for mum? She can count the number of her dinner guests and simply retrieve the required number of portions from her freezer. She can lay these in the bottom of a casserole dish, cover with a can of a chicken sauce mix like coq-au-vin, and bake for a couple of hours. This leaves her time to clean the house, have a bath, do her hair and get her make-up on before the arrival of the guests.

The portions are not done for the convenience of the housewife. Plenty of poultry in the factory farming world come down with ulcers, abscesses, gangrene and wounds caused by fighting each other for space in a cramped barn. Nobody would buy a chicken that had a fucking great abscess on one breast but they would buy its legs, wings, and its other breast. Or products made from the flesh scraped off its carcass.

Sean didn't like it in Portions. It smelled worse than anywhere in the factory. He tried not to look at the waste bins full of amputated flesh. He couldn't help it though. He always felt his eyes being drawn to them and his throat clicking in readiness for the dry retch when he catches sight of a particularly gruesome cyst. He'd hate to work here again. One Christmas he'd worked here for a week. It had fucked up his Christmas dinner. He couldn't eat the turkey. All he could see was pus from a volcanic mound with a deep hole in the centre.

And the smell of rotten meat. He was off his chicken for six months. It wasn't till he was drunk one night and had a Kentucky that he realised he could eat chicken again. But he'd never work here again, that's for sure.

He grabbed his gloves tightly, and eyes front, back erect, left, left, left-right-left, he went through the plastic curtains and was in the clean air of the corridor outside Frozen.

CHAPTER 6

Frozen was as cold as sunrise in the prairie. The frost-white American flatlands going on for ever. On it stands a yellow farmhouse with a yard and a barn. They're big buildings made out of wood. At this time of the morning there's nothing much happening. The homesteader got up before dawn. He put his dungarees on and came stretching into the kitchen. He made himself a coffee and ate some sort of corn-based bread product. He put the dishes in the sink for his wife and went out to check the fields. The sky was just turning blue, waiting for the sun that would thaw the earth. Clouds of smoke left his mouth as he scanned his kingdom. He didn't see any outlaws. Just the new telegraph line disappearing into the expanse. He adjusted his hat and crossed the yard. The cold bit into his ears and nose. His boots rattled on the hard ground. He entered the barn. Frost sparkled on the walls and floor. In the distance he could see blue images of men bent over cardboard boxes. He could hear forklifts beep beep beep before they appeared behind flashing amber lights. He blew hot steam into his hands and clapped and rubbed them together. He called Sammy and one of the blurred forms stood up and walked towards him.

Alright wee man? How ye doin?

Sean banged his hands together.

It's fuckin cold in here eh?

Sammy rubbed his red nose.

Aye pal. What are ye after?

Sean looked up and down Frozen.

Four packets of Golden Virginia.

Gie's a score.

Him on the market will gie me five packets for that.

Sammy's eyes narrowed.

Well go to him then.

Sean kicked at a bit of frozen chicken fat stuck to the floor.

Ah would but Ah thought as yer Archie's pal and that Ah could do worse.

Sammy laughed.

Yer as bad as him. Gie me twenty quid and Ah'll gie ye five packets.

Ah want some bevvy as well.

What are ye after?

Two bottles of Smirnoff.

Cost ye another tenner.

Ah'll gie ye a fiver.

Sammy growled.

Yer bein fuckin cheeky now.

Alright. Ah'm only messin. Tenner it is.

Gies the moncy then and Ah'll sort out yer stuff in the canteen at dinner time. Ye'll be able to slip it straight into yer bag.

Sean pulled three ten-pound notes out his pocket and held them out. Sammy looked up and down the warehouse before he took them.

So, are ye lookin forward to the night? said Sammy.

What, to another night in front of the telly?

Are ye no havin a wee celebration drink with me and Archie?

What are ye on about?

He's out the day.

Sean's reply was drowned by the beeping of an approaching forklift. They had to squeeze against the side of the wall to let it past. The driver gave Sammy the fingers and winked at Sean. Sammy said what in a hot spray into Sean's ear. Sean pulled his face away from the smell of Golden Virginia and bad teeth and saw the red skin eating into Sammy's silver earring. Sean leaned on the wall.

The day?

Sammy laughed at the good news he was passing on.

Bet ye cannay wait to see him eh?

Aye it's goin to be some night.

Sammy gave Sean a quizzical look.

Ah thought ye'd be pleased.

Sean tried to look pleased.

Aye Ah am.

Ye don't look it wee man.

Sean nodded.

Ah am. Ah'm just shocked. That's all. Ah thought he wasnay out till July.

Aye well he's out the day.

How come?

The jammy cunt got six months knocked off coz he agreed to come out on a tag.

But he never telt me when Ah spoke to him at Christmas.

Must've been wantin to surprise ye.

He's full of surprises.

Sammy nodded with a smile.

He is that.

So when are we expecting him?

Sammy looked at his watch.

His train'll be leavin Edinburgh any time now.

That's magic. So Ah'll be seein him the night.

Ye'll be seein him before that.

How come?

He telt me yeez have got a wee bit of business to catch up with before he does anythin.

Aye well he knows where Ah live.

He does that alright.

Sean pushed himself off the wall.

Right, Ah better get back to work.

Aye. Ah'll see ye in the canteen.

Sammy.

Aye son.

Ah've no got a fag to my name. Could ye spare me a couple till later?

Sammy pulled out a packet of tailor-mades. Sean took two. He put one in his mouth and the other behind his ear and pushed through the plastic curtains into the corridor. He couldn't face another walk through Portions. He decided to nip out the fire door so he could have a smoke and a think in the fresh air. The alarm had been fucked for weeks so nobody would know.

He pushed the bars on the door and flinched as the sun hit him. It was like opening the curtains on a whisky hangover. He trudged through the snow to a sheltered bit beneath an overhanging roof. He leaned against the wall with his wrist over his eyes. He lit his fag and looked at bits of plastic bag caught in the barbed wire fence. Cigarette ends lay at his feet. Steam leaked from pipes and dripping condensation eroded holes in the snow. His shoulders fell deeper into the wall with every suck on his cigarette. Archie's out today.

Ah'm fucked.

Archie'll have a clear plastic bag with HMP wrote on it and a travel warrant in his back pocket. He'll be standing on the platform at Waverley looking like some class of outlaw from the cowboy films. One of them guys that's going to rape loads of women and kill loads of men before him and the good guy have a gun battle at the end. And then he goes down. He bucks with every bullet hit, drops his gun as he falls to the floor, and curses the world before he dies.

Archie waits for the next train to Glasgow. And here it comes, gliding into the station, stopping with a squeak beside him. He looks up at the castle and steps into a carriage. He swings his bag in front of him as he makes his way between the seats. He finds an empty one facing forward with a big table to put his stuff on. The train leaves with a shudder and Archie tells the guy across the corridor to look after his bag while he goes to the buffet for a beer. He comes back and sits down and lights up a fag. As they fly westward he looks out the window and plans what he's going to do with his money.

Fuck sake.

Archie'll turn up with a thirst that would choke a horse. He'll want to stay. He'll want his money. They'll be junkies phoning the house every five minutes looking for him. Lassies phoning up claiming they're pregnant by him. The polis trying to do Sean for conspiracy so he'll grass Archie up. Old pals from the jail turning up looking for a bed for the night. Maggie'll be telling Sean to tell Archie to leave.

Jesus Christ.

A robin landed on a fence post and looked at him. Its tail twitched and it took its weight on and off its skinny little legs. It rubbed its beak on the post, had a last look at Sean, and flew off to the woods or somewhere.

*

When Archie came out of Glenochil he was full of ideas. He telt me life in Royston was shite and we didnay need to put up with it. We could fuckin do anythin. We just needed to want it enough. He telt me the guys in the jail had showed him how to do all sorts of useful stuff like sortin car alarms so ye could steal a better class of motor. And how to get DVLA documents so ye could sell the cunt instead of just drivin it about for a night or two. It sounded impressive to me.

Ah loved bein Archie's brother then. Ah'd get wee

bits of hash for nothin. The odd coupla pound. Sometimes Ah'd go into school and older lads would gie me fags. But the best was when he came down to the youth club with Sammy and telt me and Gambo about his exploits. It sounded like the sort of life Ah wanted. He held his fist up when he telt us about this university lassie he'd gave a bit of rough to. We looked at each other and nodded. Archie said he done things her usual boyfriends wouldnay even think about. Then he pulled fifty quid from his pocket and telt us the students were loaded. They would appear from all over the country. From nice families where the da's a lawyer and the ma's a teacher. They would want to experience a bit of the big city. Maybe even get a wee bit of draw. Thing is they were too feart to nip down to Possil to get it themselves. So that's where Ah come in.

We looked at each other and nodded. Then he gave us a pound and telt us we'd seen nothin. Ah said Aye and Gambo looked at them with his mouth open. Archie said he was off and Sammy followed him out of the door. Yer brother's mental said Gambo when they'd left. Ah winked at him and said yer fuckin right he is. Ah was proud as fuck.

Most nights Archie would get his dinner and disappear. Ah'd have to leave the window open for him and Ah'd only know he'd came home coz he was in the bed in the mornin. Sometimes there would be videos or stereos in the room. Once he came in and Ah was lookin at a video Ah'd found under the bed. Ah didnay notice him comin in and he gave me a hard punch on the top of the head. It was fuckin agony. Then he telt me it was for my own good coz if the polis were to find my dabs on the video Ah'd go to the jail. And he didnay think Ah could handle the jail. And what if Albert had came in? he said, and gave me another dig.

My uncle said he should get his head out his arse and get a job. Archie telt him workin was for mugs. Albert soon got sick of comin home from work with Archie still in his bed.

Ah came back from school one afternoon and bumped into Sammy on his way to get Archie. We went into the house and my uncle was sittin at the kitchen table with a can of beer in his hand. Ye could tell he'd had a hard day in the factory coz he had that get out my sight look in his eyes. Sammy said hiya and Albert grunted. Sammy looked at me with a frown but Ah just looked away.

Then Archie came into the kitchen. His hair was all over the place and he was rubbin his eyes. He asked my auntie Jessie to make him a cup of tea. A cup of fuckin tea shouted my uncle. Sammy backed towards the kitchen door. So did Ah. Last thing Ah wanted was a right-hander off my uncle when he had a drink in him. But Archie wasnay feart. He walked over to my uncle and stood in front of him starin right into his eyes. Albert went to hit him but Archie had learned a trick or two in the jail. It was fuckin horrible. They ended up rollin around on the kitchen floor knockin lumps out of each other. The table and chairs got scattered everywhere. Albert started to get the better of him and was puttin the boot in till my auntie screamed for him to stop and dragged him back. Archie stood up and limped to the kitchen door. Then he turned round and pointed. Ah'll beat ye the next time ya old bastard. He nodded at Sammy and the two of them left the house. Albert rubbed his bloody nose and telt me and my auntie Jessie never to let that ungrateful wee cunt back in the house.

★

Sean took a last puff on his fag and dropped it at his feet. He stood on it and walked round the walls and into the factory at the loading bay.

He nipped into Rab's shed. Rab was still sitting reading a magazine. He looked up and laughed.

Back again. D'ye want a look at my scud book?

No Ah want to use the phone.

Rab pointed to the phone on his desk.

Go ahead.

Sean hesitated.

But it's a private call.

Rab picked his fags off the desk. He nodded at the phone.

Right, Ah'm goin for a smoke. Knock yerself out.

Sean picked up the phone and dialled the number.

Clydesdale Bank. Anna speaking.

Hello. Can Ah speak to the manager?

Have you got an account here?

Aye.

Could I have your details?

Sean gave them to her. She told him to hold. Sean waited.

I'm afraid he's busy at the moment. Could I take a message?

Ah need to see him. It's urgent.

Hang on.

Sean waited again. She came back on.

The manager is very busy Mr O'Grady. You could come into the branch to see his assistant Mr Mulvey.

When?

Ten past ten?

Nice one doll. Ah'll see ye then.

Sean left the shed and called to Rab.

Cheers son.

No bother Sean. Ah'll see ye at break.

Sean hurried through Fresh. A quick nod to George and he was up the stairs and into the Junction. The white cap had a bit of a sweat on but he was coping alright. Sean tapped his shoulder.

Cheers son.

The boy left and Sean attacked the chickens that were falling on his conveyor belt. He had timed it just right. They were reaching their mid-morning crescendo. Sean got into them two-handed. As his right hung a chicken on a hook, his left grabbed another.

The machine clicked and hissed faster and faster. Sean focused on the piles of chickens clogging up his station. He felt like someone had placed the weight of all the chickens in all the world on his back. He felt like an old man. He could see what was in store for him.

An eternity of this fuckin shite.

Chickens piled on his station like debts. They reached the edge of the belt and even started falling on the floor.

He sucked the stink through his nose and attacked the pile. He pulled them out with such force he could feel the hips dislocating.

Come here ya bastards.

He sweated and puffed as he faced the landslide of chickens. He would be buried and it would take the pit rescue blokes three weeks to pull his dead body from the rotten pile. Neighbours and relatives would gather by the factory doors leaving wreath after wreath to the memory of a crushed hero. There would be cameras from the BBC and a wee honey that used to work on the weather telling the country about the size of the catastrophe. Mr O'Grady lived in Royston. He leaves a distraught wife and a daughter. He'll be missed.

CHAPTER 7

Did ye get the baccy?

Ah'm pickin it up in the canteen at break.

Albert leaned on a post next to Sean's station.

So what was Sammy sayin to it?

Ye know what he's like.

Aye, full of shite.

He keeps ye gassin for ever.

About fuck-all Ah bet ye.

Sean looked up.

He telt me Archie was out the day.

Albert didn't say anything.

Did ye hear me?

Aye. How come we don't know about it?

Exactly.

Ye think the boy would tell his family first so we could get ready for him.

Aye Ah know.

Albert smiled.

But maybe he wanted to surprise us.

Sean never said anything.

Are ye alright? said Albert.

Sean nodded and looked at the floor.

There's somethin up. Ah can tell.

Sean pulled himself upright and had a deep breath.

It's eh –

What?

Sean breathed out.

Ah, nothin.

What's the matter with ye?

Sean stared at the floor

Never mind.

Ah'm no such an old cunt Ah wouldnay help my favourite nephew.

Ah know. It's just –

Albert put his hand on Sean's shoulder.

What's up?

Don't worry about it.

Come on son. A problem shared is a problem halved.

Sean pulled away from Albert.

Aye right.

Albert gave Sean his fuck ye look.

Don't say Ah didnay try.

Ah'd never say that. Yer tryin alright.

Ha fuckin ha.

Sean rubbed his hands together.

Ah don't know what's happened to the break.

Albert gazed into the distance.

Aye. It'll soon be time for a fried breakfast and a cup of tea.

Sean rubbed his belly.

Cannay wait.

We should get ready to go. Get down there at the top of the queue.

Ah'll be gettin mine a bit after.

Why's that?

Ah've got a wee bit of business to sort out before Ah can have my dinner.

George came in and told them they could go. Sean told Albert he'd see him in the canteen and ran for the stairs. He ran straight into the swarm at the door shouting make way for the Emperor. He pushed and jinked and excuse me'd until he was at the head of the crowd pouring into the canteen. He clocked Sammy in the corner booth with his arm up on the side, foot on the table, and a white cap retreating with a clinking plastic bag. As Sean got close to the table, Sammy took a draw on his roll-up and put his arm on the back of the chair where his punters sat. He nodded at Sean.

Alright? said Sean.

No bad.

Have ye got my stuff?

Sammy pulled a bag from under the table. Sean grabbed it and stood up.

Cheers Sammy Ah'll see ye later.

Sean went through Fresh and into Packing. He found Rab in his shed with his head stuck in the same magazine.

Ya dirty wee bastard. Ye'll go blind.

Rab jumped.

Fuck sake, Ah thought ye were George.

Sean held up his bag.

Will ye look after this for us?

Aye no bother.

Sean put it under Rab's desk.

Cheers son. Help yerself to a wee drink of the voddy.

Ah'll maybe just do that.

No too much but. Yer da'll kill me if he catches ye.

Right.

Ah'll get it off ye on the bus.

Sean left Packing and headed for the exit. He nodded to the security guard on the way out of the main gates. It was nice to get out of the stink and into the fresh country air. His appointment with the man at the Clydesdale was ten past ten. Five past now. Plenty of time. Sean liked this part of the town. The old houses with their thatched roofs. The black beams that criss-crossed the facias. The leaded windows. He could just imagine a horse and cart with a pile of rosy red apples in the back and a tasty country bit on the front seat. One of them fat lassies with red cheeks and a smile on her face. Maybe a front tooth missing so you know you're in the old days. The clip clop echoing down the narrow street. Maybe a guy walking past with a scythe over his shoulder and a bit of straw hanging out of his mouth.

Sean spat onto the mucky snow at the side of the road. It was cold out. He bent forward into the wind and pulled the peak of his cap down over his forehead. Just as well he had his freezer jacket on. A pensioner struggled up the pavement with a bag full of shopping. Tears ran out of her eyes. Her shoes had a split in the side and she walked with a grimace.

He climbed the wide steps into the bank. Big white pillars framed the doorway. You could tell it used to be a rich cunt's house. Some guy that made a fortune in the tobacco game. Or maybe from weaving clothes for the army or the prison service. The autobank machine cut into the side of the wall gave the game away. They didn't have them back then. Sean wondered if they made the hole special or they fitted it into a doorway. Or a window.

He went into the perfumed heat of the bank. There was a queue at the tellers but for once he didn't have to wait in it. He went straight to the receptionist's desk. An attractive lassie glanced up and looked down at him.

Can I help you?

Ah've come to see Mr Mulvey.

The receptionist had a good look at his fat-splattered overalls.

Take a seat and I'll find out if he's available.

He better be coz Ah've got an appointment.

Sean sat down and watched the receptionist get buzzed into the interior of the bank.

Huffy cow.

Sean took off his cap and picked bits of chicken from it. He rolled them up like snotters and flicked them on the carpet. Then he folded his cap up and squeezed it into his pocket. He picked at some bobbles on the chair. They came loose with a scratch.

A guy in a grey suit came out of the office.

Mr O'Grady?

Sean stood up and shook the outstretched hand.

Come through.

He followed Mulvey into his office.

What can I do for you?

Ah need a lend of some money.

Mulvey looked at Sean's overalls.

Yes? And how much would you like to borrow?

Sean felt like a wee boy up in front of the head.

Seven hunner pound.

That's a lot of money.

Well it's what Ah need.

Indeed. And may I ask why you require the loan?

Why?

Yes Mr O'Grady. Why?

Sean looked at the carpet.

Ah want to buy a motor.

Mulvey frowned.

Loans for leisure purposes can be difficult to obtain.

Sean fidgeted in his chair.

It's no just leisure. Ah'll use it to get to work and back.

Mulvey tapped his teeth with his pen.

I'll just consult the branch manager.

Mulvey got up and left the office. Sean watched the clock click. It was warm in the office and he still had his freezer jacket on. He stretched his legs out. He sighed. He crossed his arms over his chest.

C'mon to fuck.

The clock clicked. He looked out the window. There was a walled garden with shrubs round the edge of a lawn. Someone had built a bird table in the middle of the lawn. It had a sack of nuts hanging from it. Sean watched the starlings grab bits of bread and fly off to little private dens for a quiet chew. A fat pigeon pecked the crumbs the starlings dropped on the lawn. Sean wondered if a cat ever came in and caught one of the birds. Jumped up and batted it to the floor then sunk its teeth right into the back of the neck. A pile of feathers and bits of down and the carcass left lonely in the winter sun.

★

The night Archie crippled that skinhead was the same night Ah met Maggie. Gambo had asked if Ah wanted to go to the youth club disco with him. He said there would be lassies from all over and Ah had a chance of grabbin one of them. He came round mine that night and we were combin our hair in the livin room mirror when Archie said Ah couldnay pull in a barrel of fannies. My uncle Albert laughed. My auntie Jessie said they were bein disgustin and telt me to never mind them. Just go and enjoy yerself son. Aye go and enjoy yerself said Archie and nudged my uncle. They both laughed. Ah couldnay wait to get out the house.

We were walkin down Cadge Road and Gambo said c'mon Sean hurry up. Ah looked ahead and there was two lassies comin out a house. Gambo shouted Lizzie and they waited for us to catch up. Gambo fancied Lizzie and she fancied him so they walked on ahead and left me and Maggie to it. It was pretty handy coz Maggie was a wee honey, so she was.

When we got to the disco Maggie and her sister disappeared into the toilets. Gambo reckoned he was right in there. He asked me if Ah thought Ah had a chance with Maggie. Ah said Ah didnay know. He said he heard her laugh when Ah was talkin to her and that was a good sign. We went to the bar and bought a can of Coke each and drunk some of it. Then Ah pulled a half bottle of voddy out my jacket and poured some into the cans. We leaned against the wall and watched what was goin on.

There was a gang of older guys from the school hangin about so Ah was a bit shy when Ah went to the toilet in case they followed me in and took my drink off me. One of them was a skinhead. He was bigger than the others and had the same dot on his face as Archie. Ah didnay want to look at him. Best thing Ah could do was stay out his way.

After a few swigs on the voddy but, Ah got a bit brave. Then next time Ah walked past the gang of them Ah looked the skin right in the eye. He drew his finger across his neck. Ah kept starin at him and made my eyes go cocked. He sprung towards me but his pals grabbed him and pulled him back.

When Ah got back to where Gambo was he called me a prick. Asked me what the fuck Ah thought Ah was doin. Said Ah was goin to get the pair of them a kickin. Ah telt him no to be a big woman then Ah went up to Maggie and asked her for a dance. She said aye and we had a wee jig. Then we went to the bar and Ah bought her a Coke. Ah offered her a bit of voddy. She had a wee bit but said she'd have to watch in case her dad smelt it coz he'd kill her.

Walk on the Wild Side came on and Ah asked her if she fancied it. We danced and Ah pushed my face against her head and smelled her hair. Ah pulled her close and she pushed her belly against me. We had a kiss and Ah started to get a root so Ah pulled myself away from her and led her to the side of the hall. Ah looked at Gambo and winked.

Then Archie and Sammy turned up. They'd been on the glue and the youth club leader didnay want to let them in but he never had much choice. They started pogoin through the slow dances and pushin couples apart. Ah saw Sammy spittin on some lassie and pushin her boyfriend to the ground when he objected. There was an odd shoe lyin on the floor. Ah saw the guy behind the bar on the phone and Ah knew it was time to go, but with the skin and his pals about the place it was best for me to stay near Archie.

One of the skinhead's pals pushed his way through the dancin and started fightin with Sammy. Next thing the skin and his other pal went for Archie. Ma brother was doin alright but. He put the skin's pal down with a head-butt followed by a kick in the balls. But then the skin stroked him right on the jaw with a bottle. Archie bent over, holdin his bloody face. The skin kicked him one in the guts and Ah thought it was all over. So Ah ran in there but Ah got knocked over by a bang on the side of the head and ended up at the edge of the dance floor bein comforted by Maggie. She held my head in her lap like Ah was some sort of wounded cowboy.

My wee attack gave Archie enough time to pick up a chair and smash it right into the skinhead's face. It knocked the cunt to the floor. Archie didnay stop at that but. He crashed the chair into the skin's head and back until it fell to bits. By the time the polis turned up he was layin still. They grabbed Archie, and Sammy ran into them, arms flailin everywhere. It didnay take them long to settle him down.

Sammy did alright but, coz the judge only gave him a year for affray. Our Archie got three years for serious assault. The judge said he was a menace to society. Archie was well chuffed. He turned round from the dock and winked at me. He wasnay so chuffed though when he was shipped to a prison up in the Highlands.

The first time we visited him he said he was proud of me for what Ah'd done. It was great sittin there with my uncle and my big brother and both of them sayin Ah was some guy. Ah walked out of that jail with a swagger and a half, and an idea that one day me and Archie would do a bit of time the gether. That we'd be tobacco barons and live in a cell filled with nude books and records and grovelling prisoners.

But on the way home Albert had a word with me. He said it's alright bein a big hard man and that, but fightin needs to be kept in its place. Some of the time it might be needed, but it should only be used when all else fails. It wasnay to be abused and enjoyed. When that happened, the fists ruled with the man and no the other way about. And we know where that leads.

The fuckin jail. And plenty of it.

But anyway, he could see Ah wasnay like Archie. Best thing Ah could do from now on was stick in at the school and make sure Ah stayed out of trouble with the polis.

★

The door opened and Mulvey stepped back into the office. He walked across the floor and didn't look at Sean until the desk was between them.

Mr O'Grady. We've looked at the figures and I'm sorry but I don't think there's anything we can do for you.

Sean tried to smile. He rubbed his sweaty hands up and down his thighs.

OK.

Mulvey shuffled some more papers.

If you keep your account in credit and come back and see me in six months I'm sure we'll look upon your application more positively.

OK.

Mulvey stood up. He extended his hand.

See you in six months then.

Sean shook Mulvey's hand and left the office. He kept his eye on the pattern of the carpet and almost walked into an old lady.

Eh sorry.

You should watch where you're going young man.

Sean looked at her.

Fuck off.

He heard a gasp from a woman stood next to the old one so he gave her a look that dared her to say anything. The woman looked away and Sean barged out of the bank and back into the cold. He crunched through the snow on the way back to work. The sound of his wellies reverberated round the street and inside his head. What the fuck was he going to do now? He stopped in a doorway to roll a fag. A nice big fat one. He lit it, cupped it in his hand, and re-entered the wind. A couple of puffs and the wind lifted a bit of ash and it flew right into his eye.

For fuck sake.

Sean protected his eye from the wind by turning to face a wall and holding up his hands. He blinked and blinked and felt the bit of ash score into his eyeball. He kicked the wall. Eventually he managed to get the shit out and carried on to his work. By the time he got there, tears were running down his cheek. The security guard looked up from his paper and asked Sean what was the matter.

Mind yer own business.

Ah'm only askin son.

Sean stomped through the gates and into the factory. He went to the toilet and gave his eye a good wash out at the sink. Then he patted it with a bit of tissue paper. It wasn't as itchy now so he thought he'd be able to manage going to the canteen without anybody else asking him what was the matter.

Shower of nosy bastards he said to his reflection.

He left the toilet and went to the canteen. The queue was pretty short when he got there. At ten o'clock it's huge but by this time most people have had their breakfast and are settling into a cup of tea and a fag. He grabbed a tray and slid it along the rails. The baldy guy behind the counter grabbed a plate off the pile by the side of the till and nodded at Sean.

What can Ah get ye?

Fried breakfast.

Crispy bacon?

Ye've got me sussed.

The baldy guy gave Sean a shy wee smile. Sean wondered if he was a poof. As the guy bent over to slide a fried egg onto his spatula, Sean saw a bead of sweat gather on his head and make its way towards his forehead. It joined another bead just above his eyebrows. They raced down his nose and hung there for a second before dropping right onto Sean's fried egg.

No that one.

What?

Ah don't want that fried egg.

What's up with it?

Ah don't want it.

Why?

Just put it back. Ah don't fuckin want it. Alright?

OK. Keep yer hair on.

Aye alright, just gie's another egg.

The baldy guy put a fresh egg on Sean's plate. Then a sausage and two rashers of bacon.

Beans or tomatoes?

How long have Ah been comin here?

Sorry Sean, tomatoes it is.

Don't forget the toast.

Sean took the plate and put it on his tray. He slid it along the rails and picked up a mug of tea. Then he went to the till, paid for his breakfast and looked round the canteen for Albert. The old guy waved and Sean pushed through the tables to sit next to his uncle.

Ye still look miserable son.

Sean cut a piece of sausage and dipped it into his egg yolk. He felt like he was ten again and his uncle was asking him if he'd done his homework.

What's the matter?

Sean ate his breakfast and did nothing to communicate with Albert except shake his head and point at his plate. Albert sat back in his seat and rolled a fag. Sean felt him watching as the breakfast found its way into his belly. He scrunched up the toast and rubbed the egg yolk and tomato juice from the plate.

Where've ye been? said Albert.

Sean swallowed a mouthful of bacon and toast.

Ah had to nip down the bank.

Oh aye?

Sean ignored the question and speared the last piece of sausage and wiped it round the egg yolk drying on the plate. He took his time chewing it and sucking out the juices before he swallowed it. He dropped the fork and knife onto his plate and wiped his mouth with the back of his hand.

Enjoy that? said Albert

Fuckin lovely.

Sean slurped a big mouthful of tea. He rolled a roll-up, sat back with a burp and a sigh and lit up his fag. Albert looked at him.

So what's been getting ye down the day?

It's Archie.

What about him?

Sean took a drag on his fag. He looked to make sure no one was listening. He started to whisper.

He gave me some money to look after for him.

Albert started to whisper.

How much?

A thousand.

Albert looked around him to make sure no one was listening.

And ye've spent it?

Just about.

Albert scratched his head.

How much?

Seven hunner.

What did ye spend it on?

That school trip for Donna.

Albert looked Sean right in the eye.

That was a dear fuckin trip.

Sean looked at the table.

Eh no just that. Christmas as well.

Albert blew a big puff of smoke towards the ceiling.

Some Christmas that must've been.

Sean didn't know where to look.

Aye.

Albert had another slow puff on his fag.

So that's what ye've been doin the overtime for?

Aye. Ah thought Ah could get the cash the gether before he got out in July.

Best-laid plans eh?

Aye.

He's goin to be fuckin angry.

Sean bit his lip.

Ah know.

So what did the bank say?

They werenay much help.

They never are.

Fuckin bastards. Ah've been with that bank for years.

They're like that son. Only interested in lendin ye money if ye've already got plenty.

Archie's goin to fuckin kill me.

But ye've no spent all his money. Three hunner is better than nothin.

It'll no be enough to stop him kickin my arse.

Albert had a puff on his fag and nodded through the smoke.

Looks like yer in fuckin trouble son.

Ah need to get more money.

Albert leaned back into his chair and tried to take another draw on his fag. It took a couple of puffs to get it going then he had a deep drag that gave him a coughing fit. He pulled out a hanky and wiped his lips.

Ah'll see what Ah can do.

What do ye mean?

Ah'll phone yer auntie Jessie and see if we can gie ye a loan.

Albert paused then spoke some more.

Ah doubt we'll be able to get ye the lot but we'll gie ye some of it.

No Ah couldnay do that.

How no?

It wouldnay be right.

Albert put his hand on Sean's arm.

We're family son.

Sean leaned on the table with his forehead on his wrist.

This is doin my fuckin nut in.

Albert ruffled Sean's hair.

Ah know son.

Ah'll no let ye down Albert.

Ye better no or yer auntie'll kill me.

They put their fags out and got up from the table. A quick trip to the toilet and they were back in the Junction counting chickens.

CHAPTER 8

Albert?

Aye pal?

Ye'll no believe this.

What?

Ah've just counted sixty-seven seconds between two chickens.

Sixty-seven?

Aye sixty-fuckin-seven.

Is that a record for ye the day?

Fuckin right it is.

Albert picked a chicken off the belt and hung it on a hook.

D'ye think it'll stay a record?

Course it will. Sixty-seven long seconds. Put that in yer pipe and smoke it.

Ah would but smokin shite gies me a sore throat.

Jealous eh?

Of course Ah am. Sixty-seven seconds is a great achievement.

Fuck off ya sarky old cunt.

Albert laughed.

Ah'm messin with ye. Sixty-seven's no a bad score.

Sean held a chicken up like a trophy and shook it by the wings.

No bad? It's pure fuckin champion.

It's no quite champion son.

How d'ye mean?

Albert pushed his cheek out with his tongue.

It's no as good as seventy-three.

When did ye get seventy-three?

Ah got that between two Sunday roasters before we went for breakfast.

Aye right.

Ah'm serious.

What, really?

Albert breathed on his hand and rubbed it on his shoulder.

Aye. Seventy-three.

Bet ye counted fast.

Albert pointed at Sean.

No as fast as you ya wee cunt.

Ah count slow ya old bastard.

Yer too tight to count slow.

Ah used my watch.

Albert turned his back.

Liar.

Aye Ah know ye are.

Sean grabbed a chicken and banged it on a hook. Twenty-three till the next one. Then he counted eighty-six.

Albert?

What is it now?

Eighty-six.

What?

Eighty-fuckin-six.

Eighty-six what?

Eighty-six between two chickens.

Yer telling lies so ye are.

No. Eighty-six seconds.

Maggie'll be pleased.

Ya old prick. Yer just gutted coz Ah've broke yer record.

Albert pointed at the door.

Away into personnel and pick up yer medal.

Fuck off.

Sean picked up another chicken and placed it on its hook. He heard Scotland the Brave playing as he leaned forward to receive his medal from some royal princess with blonde hair and a silk shirt on. Or maybe a movie-star type or a Miss World. He saw the cleavage as she bent to place the medal round his neck. She gave him a smile and he knew it was game on when he saw her later in the bar. His auntie Jessie watched from the stadium. She wiped a tear from her cheek. Albert was tight-lipped and his eyes were shining. What a day for Scotland and the O'Gradys. What a day.

Sean, called Albert across the Junction.

What is it?

Ah've got an idea about Archie.

Sean looked around. He walked over to Albert.

What?

Ye could ask yer pal Gambo for a wee hand.

Sean picked at his gloves.

Ah couldnay do that.

How no?

Sean looked at Albert as if he was daft.

Ye know.

Ye shouldnay let that bother ye.

Tell that to Archie.

He doesnay need to know.

Aye maybe.

Albert turned to pick up a fallen chicken.

Ye've known the guy since ye were weans, so it's no outrageous to ask him for a wee hand. Is it?

Aye but Ah could be puttin him in a position he doesnay want to be in.

Ye could just ask him for a bit of advice.

Ah've no really spoke to him since the weddin.

Maybe it's about time ye did.

Sean heard a chicken land on his station, so he nipped over and then came back to Albert.

But what would Ah say to him?

Just tell him what ye've done and how worried ye are.

But he'll think Ah'm a prick.

So?

But –

A chicken landed on Albert's station.

How much do ye want out of this mess?

Sean pulled the peak of his cap.

Alright. Alright. Ah'll ask him.

Albert patted Sean on the arm.

That's my boy. It's goin to be alright.

D'ye think so?

Albert never said anything for a while, then he nodded.

It'll be alright. Ah'll get ye some money and ye can put that in with what ye've got. Ye can speak to yer pal and see what he can do for ye. Before ye know it we'll be sittin back and laughin at all the fuckin panic.

Sean looked left and right like a child doing the Green Cross Code.

Aye but if Archie finds out Ah've even thought about goin to Gambo, he'll fuckin kill me.

Maybe that's a risk ye'll need to take.

A chicken landed on Sean's station. By the time he got over there the machine was dropping loads and he didn't get the chance to finish their blether. He pulled them apart like an army NCO breaking up a wrestle. Big chest and shoulders pushing in amongst the skinny recruits, grabbing collars and arms and dishing out the odd punch. Before long the rioters would be scattered and subdued. Sitting on their bunks nursing bruises. A cheeky one would try and say something but the big sergeant would just look at him and the wee cunt would shut up and sit down. Failing that he'd knock the boy to the floor. Harmony would be restored to the barracks. Sergeant O'Grady could put his cap over his face and dream of his comfortable life back home with the missus.

Albert's voice kept coming into Sean's head. Ask him. Ask Gambo for help. Never mind the consequences. Just ask him. When Sean finished work he'd get straight on the phone and tell Gambo everything that's been going on. From the time Archie sent Sammy round with the DSS envelope full of twenties, right up till the other

97

week when he took a note for a punt at the bookies. Gambo would help. He knows what it's like to make a wee mistake and have a pal bail you out.

*

It was really sunny, so me and Gambo decided to dog the school for the day. We went in for registration then jumped the back fence when the rest of them went to double English. As long as we didnay get into any trouble, nobody would know we werenay in the school.

It was some laugh walkin down the road towards the city centre. We kidded on we were Russian spies in Glesga to check for places to print money and passports. Every time we saw a motor we'd duck into the hedges so they couldnay see us. Gambo reckoned he knew a brilliant wee hideout as we walked down The Avenues. We looked up and down the street, jumped over a wall, across a lawn and through a hedge, and we came to a shed in this overgrown garden. Ye could tell it was some old dear's house coz the windows were manky and there was one of them flowery aprons hangin from the washin line. Gambo said his ma was the old dear's home help but we didnay need to worry coz it was her day off and she wouldnay be back till the morra.

We settled into the shed by movin the lawnmower and gettin two deckchairs off the wall. After five minutes sittin in the chairs goin this is alright we got up and had a look through the tins of stuff that were layin

around. Paint and thinners and old tools. Gambo reckoned we could get some money for the tools but Ah
couldnay see it. We put some in a plastic bag though,
just in case.

When we'd had a good look through everythin, we
started throwin bits of spider's web at each other. Ah
rubbed some in Gambo's hair and he called me a dirty
bastard and pushed me onto a deckchair. The canvas
split and Ah ended up with my arse on the floor. We
had a bit of a laugh at that but the shed was gettin
roastin so we decided to go out for some fresh air. We'd
maybe come back if it rained. Gambo made me swear
on my auntie Jessie's life that Ah wouldnay tell anybody
about the hideout.

Once we were on the street we took turns at brushin
the bits of dust and web off each other's clothes. Then
we took the tools to a secondhand shop in Magdalene
Street. There was a plane and a set of chisels in the bag.
It wasnay that heavy but it was a long walk so it started
to drag on my arm by the time we got there. Gambo
didnay know where to go. Ah said we should try
Sparky's. Ah remember Archie sayin he'd sold him a
stereo and got good money for it.

A bell went when we pushed the door open. It stunk
of damp and fags in the shop. An old guy came through
from the back. He had half an unlit roll-up hangin out
his mouth. Let's see what ye've got he said. We went to
the counter and Gambo got the stuff out the bag. No
a lot of call for tools these days said the old guy. Ah
was gutted. All that way for nothin. Then he said he'd
gie us a pound for the lot. Gambo said aye but Ah

thought we should ask for more so Ah telt the guy they were my da's tools and he'd said we shouldnay leave the shop with less than a fiver. He laughed and said a fiver, yer in the wrong business wee man, ye should've been a fuckin comedian. Ah said fair enough, there was plenty of other shops. He telt me no to be so hasty. We could split the difference and call it three bar.

Gambo was well pleased. Kept pattin me on the back and tellin me Ah was as sharp as a farmer. Ah telt him that anybody would be sharp that lived with Archie and my uncle Albert. Gambo nodded.

We went into a paper shop and Ah asked the woman for ten Regal. She gave me a funny look so Ah telt her they were for my ma. When she turned round to get them Gambo stuffed a coupla sausage rolls up his jumper. Ah grabbed a Mars Bar and a Twix. My heart was poundin as we walked out the shop but the woman didnay say anythin. We jogged up the street until we came to a wee bench under a tree. The sausage rolls were lovely. We washed them down with a bottle of gold top milk off someone's doorstep.

Sammy was out the jail so Ah said we should go up to Sighthill and see him. Ask him how our Archie was gettin on. Sammy's ma was alright. She didnay care who went round as long as ye didnay leave fag burns on the carpet or bring the polis to the door. The bus from the city dropped us outside the block about eleven o'clock. We went up the lift and knocked on the door. Ah could hear music in the house and when the letterbox opened to ask who it was Ah could smell hash. Sammy let us in and we went to his bedroom.

Sammy and a pal were sittin in the room listenin to punk songs. He telt his pal to turn the fuckin music down. Then he said Archie was doin alright in the jail. He showed us the Dead Kennedys tattoo Archie had gave him on the forearm. It looked a bit rough but he seemed pleased enough with it. Get the fags out then he said, and Gambo gave him one. Sammy broke it up and made a joint with it. Nice bit of rocky black he said. Me and Gambo only had a coupla draws coz Sammy telt us no to hog it. He had it for ages but.

Ah asked Sammy to sell us a bit of hash for two quid. He gave us a bit but we couldnay make a joint between us so he said he'd make them for us. It didnay look like he put much in but he said ye couldnay put too much in or ye might take a whitey. His pal nodded. Whitey he said. Sammy telt us no to walk the streets smokin the joints. Ye have to watch where ye smoke them. And if ye get captured by the polis, ye didnay get the stuff off me. Me and Gambo nodded.

We stayed round there for an hour then Gambo got up off the bed and said we had to go. Sammy gave me a bag of rubbish and telt me to put it down the chute. Watch yer trousers though, coz it's drippin. There was a can of beer in it. Last thing Ah wanted was to go home stinkin of beer. We went to the bin cupboard and listened to the bag go down the chute and hit the skip at the bottom. There was a coupla concrete blocks lyin there so we put them down as well. They made some racket when they hit the skip.

When we got outside onto the forecourt Ah heard Sammy shout ye've forgot yer schoolbag ya fuckin diddy.

Ah looked up and it came flyin out the window and landed on the grass. Ah was a bit gutted coz it broke my calculator.

We went back to the old dear's shed to smoke the joints. Ah put a box under the ripped deckchair and it was pretty comfy. Gambo put on a posh accent and asked me for a light. Then he leaned back into his chair and had a few puffs. He crossed his legs and flicked a bit of ash on the floor. Ah telt him no to hog it and he passed it over. The shed was alright when ye got a joint on the go. Ah asked him what he thought of Sammy's Dead Kennedys tattoo and we burst out laughin.

Gambo got up and started pokin about with the tins of stuff on the shelves. He asked if Ah'd ever tried glue. Fuck that Ah said, that's what got our Archie into trouble. Ah asked him if he'd tried it and he said he'd had a wee blast of the Tippex. What's it like? Ah asked him. It's just like the hash he said. Only different. Ye hear a buzzin sound in yer ears then everythin goes quiet and ye wake up and it's about an hour later. Ah telt him it sounded like a lot of shite. And anyway, it might make my lungs collapse. It's good he said. He took the top off a can and had a few sniffs. Then he looked at me with this smile that didnay seem to care what was happenin. Ah thought aye why no, so Ah had a few sniffs from the top of the tin. It was good as well. Ah could hear the birds in the garden like they were down the end of a cave. Ah sparked up the other joint while Gambo blasted away at the can.

After a coupla puffs he asked to swap, so we did. One

of us must have dropped it coz the next thing Ah knew Gambo's chair was on fire. Ah woke him out his buzz and he had a coughin fit. Ah had to drag him out into the garden. It took him a coupla minutes to get his breath. Ah heard the old dear in the house shout somethin and we ran through the hedge and over the wall. We looked back and shat it coz ye could see black smoke pumpin out the garden.

We got halfway up the street before Ah realised Ah'd left my bag in the shed.

When Ah got home my auntie Jessie asked if Ah'd been playin with fires. Ah said no but she said she could smell it. Ah telt her some lads had a bonfire at the garages and Ah'd stood round it for a bit after school. But Ah hadnay put anythin in it. She telt me to stay away from fires. If ye got burned ye'd know all about it. She asked me what Ah'd been doin in school the day. Ah telt her a bit of chemistry and some physics and that. She gave me my dinner and Ah went out for a game of football on the street.

That night Ah was goin to bed and Ah heard a knock at the door. After a bit my uncle Albert gave me a shout to come downstairs. Ah went down and there was two polis in the livin room. They asked if Ah'd been to school. Ah telt them aye. Ah gave Albert the honest Ah have look. The polis asked if Ah'd been anywhere near The Avenues the day. Ah shook my head. They telt me arson was a very serious offence and carried a risk of a custodial sentence. Ah looked at my auntie and she bit her lip and looked away. My legs were shakin and Ah needed a pish. They telt me they'd found the remains of my bag in the shed. Ah started cryin and sayin it was an accident. My auntie sighed and went Sean.

The polis nodded at each other and went at me like terriers for a few minutes. Then they stood up and telt my uncle Albert to bring me down Baird Street on Monday to be formally charged. Ah would have to sign a statement and get my dabs took. If Ah was unlucky, Ah would end up in Glenochil like Archie. At the mention of that my auntie looked at me and shook her head.

Ah didnay want them to go. Ah thought Albert was goin to gie me the same whippin he'd gied Archie for the stolen car. But he never. He called me a stupid cunt. He thought Ah was different to that other useless cunt, that maybe Ah was the one in the family that had some fuckin brains. But no, it looked like brains were as short in me as they were in him. The only difference between us was Ah couldnay handle a beltin. Ah was such a big fuckin lassie he couldnay bear to hit me. Jessie said that's enough Albert. He sat in his chair and growled every coupla seconds and clenched his fists. Get to yer fuckin bed he said and Ah flinched past him and up the stairs. Ah wished he'd have gave me the belt.

It wasnay so bad though. The polis dropped the charges to Criminal Damage and all Ah got was a visit from a big sergeant who showed me pictures of people hurt in fires and hoped Ah'd learned a valuable lesson. Then a social worker turned up and she took me to the pictures once a week. She was alright. Bought me sweets and asked how Ah was gettin on at school. Gambo did alright as well. The old dear in the house had only saw one of us

so the polis thought Ah was on my own. Ah never telt
Gambo that though. He thought Ah'd got the third degree
and refused to tell them nothin. Just as well for him, coz
he'd never have got his job with a record.

★

The machine settled down to a steady beat. Sean knew
it would be easy for a while so he asked Albert to watch
his station while he went for a piss. Albert told him to
have one for me while you're there. Sean laughed and
told him he'd see him in a minute.

He rolled a fag as soon as he got in the toilet. He lit
it, took a big draw, then left it in his mouth as he pulled
his dick out and had a long, delicious pish.

Pure fuckin ecstasy man.

He shook his dick and turned round to the mirror. He
looked at his reflection and said wanker. The door to
the toilet swung open and Sammy walked in.

Alright Sammy?

Sammy went over to the pisser. His legs crooked as he
got his dick out. He half looked behind him.

Aye.

What are ye up to?

Havin a pish.

Funny.

Sammy shook his dick off and joined Sean at the basins,
where he rolled himself a fag with a wee bit of hash
crumbled into it. Sean pointed at the fag.

Ah don't know how ye can smoke that stuff at work.

It's easy, all ye do is suck it into yer mouth.

Bit of a cunny funt this mornin eh?

Sammy lit up his spliff and had a couple of double draws.
He bounced a smoke ring off the mirror.

D'ye want a wee blast?

Sean looked at the dirt under Sammy's fingernails.

No, yer alright.

Sammy nodded like a television scientist.

Gies ye a new angle on life.

Aye Ah know. But it makes me pure fuckin sleepy.

Sammy sucked his teeth with a click. Sean had a puff
on his fag and exhaled with a loud sigh. Sammy looked
at Sean and stroked his chin.

Ah was wonderin about ye this mornin.

What about me?

Ah didnay think ye'd have the balls.

What ye talkin about?

Sammy gave Sean a leer.

Ye know.

No, Ah don't.

Sean took the last couple of draws on his fag and
dropped the butt into a urinal. He went into a cubicle,
pulled a length of toilet paper and gave his nose a blow.
Sammy stayed by the basins. When Sean looked at him
again, Sammy was giving him the eye.

What?

Sammy took a long draw on his fag. He watched Sean
through the smoke.

Why did ye go to the bank this mornin?

How d'ye know Ah was at the bank?

Sammy touched the side of his nose.

Ah've got eyes and ears everywhere. Were ye there for a sub?

Mind yer own fuckin business.

Sammy licked his lips like a cat.

It's no got anythin to do with yer brother has it?

Archie?

Ye know what Ah'm talkin about.

No, Ah don't fuckin know. Why d'ye no spell it out to me?

Sammy's eyes narrowed.

Ye've spent his money.

Sean felt like a wee mouse that's just been clubbed by a big paw.

Fuck off, it's in the house.

Sammy laughed and put his hands up. He walked close to Sean and pulled his mouth into a shape that wasn't quite a smile.

Ah'm offerin ye a bit of help here wee man.

Sammy turned and walked to the wash basin. He started to wash his hands. He watched Sean in the reflection of the mirror, then he looked down into the wash basin. Sean looked at the toilet door and started walking towards it. Then he looked back at Sammy.

Yer no soundin very helpful.

Sammy looked up from his hands and smiled like a cat.

Well Ah am.

What sort of help?

The chance to get some money.

How much?

A few hunner.

That's a lot of money Sammy.

Aye it might be, but it doesnay take long to spend it.

Ha ha. So what do ye want me to do?

Ah'll tell ye later.

CHAPTER 9

Me and Maggie had been seein each other for a coupla years when Gambo turned up at Cadge Road in this motor he'd borrowed from his work. Half the neighbours were twitchin their curtains coz the noisy bastard gave the horn some beep on his way up the street. Ah ran down the garden path goin that's some motor wee man. Gambo gave me a smile that was pleased and embarrassed at the same time. D'ye fancy Largs for the weekend? he said. He'd already phoned Lizzie and she wanted to come but it would be better if me and Maggie came as well. More like Lizzie's ma wouldnay let Lizzie come without Maggie. Ah was well pleased and got straight on the phone to Maggie. She said aye, and that she had somethin to tell me anyway. Ah asked her what it was and she said she'd tell me when she saw me.

Largs is an alright wee place for a weekend away. We turned up at this B&B and the landlady was a bit funny when she saw the ages of us. She didnay know what the world was comin to when they let weans our age get married. We had a wee snigger at that. It was as if

109

the old bag had never had her hole and she was pissed off we were.

The first night there we went to the pub and had a few beers. It was a braw wee pub and ye could imagine ye were in Magaloof or somewhere eatin paella and drinkin lager. Except there were Glesga accents everywhere and all that was on the menu was plain crisps and dry roasted nuts. Then we got a bag of chips each. We took them to the beach and ate them as the sun went down over the sea. There was a coupla clouds and the sky was like torn strips of red and blue paper. Ah'd never seen anythin so spectacular.

Gambo and Lizzie got up and said they were off to the amusements. Ah didnay want to go, so me and Maggie just sat there and said cheerio to the sun. Ah knew then Ah loved her, so Ah telt her. She telt me she thought she loved me as well. But she had somethin to tell me and Ah wasnay to get upset. She looked a bit worried. Ah didnay have any idea of what she was goin to tell me. Ah was thinkin cancer or somethin, she looked that worried. Then she telt me she was pregnant. Ah didnay know what else to say, so Ah blurted out we should get married. She just nodded her head and we got up and walked over to the amusements.

Lizzie and Gambo were well pleased for us. He telt me he was thinkin of askin Lizzie but first he was goin to wait for a promotion at work. Maybe if he'd just asked her at Largs things would've turned out different.

As soon as we got back to Royston we went round my auntie and uncle's to tell them. Albert took me aside and had a word with me. Asked me why Ah wanted to get married. Ah telt him it was coz Ah loved her and wanted to settle down. But ye don't need to get married to do that he said. Ah telt him Maggie was pregnant. That shut him up for a while. Then he touched my arm and said marriage is alright son but it's no all shaggin ye know. Ah nodded as if Ah knew. But Ah didnay.

Ah wanted Archie to be my best man. He was due out the jail and a coupla weeks wasnay a long wait. Gambo was a bit gutted coz he wanted the top job himself. But Ah thought Archie's no had a lot of luck and it would gie him somethin to look forward to after the jail. We arranged to have the weddin on the last Saturday of June. Ah went to visit Archie and telt him. He was that pleased Ah was gettin married and that Ah wanted him to be my best man. Ah could see it in his eyes.

Maggie's ma and da ordered me a suit from Burtons. They even offered to buy Archie a suit but he said he'd buy his fuckin own. He got one cheap from some shady pal of his from Springburn. It was a nice suit but. More fashionable than mine. Ah was a bit jealous but my auntie Jessie telt me no to worry coz style never goes out of fashion. And that Ah was better lookin than Archie. Ah believed her. She's a good liar, my auntie Jessie.

The day itself was alright. We turned up down the registry office and done the vows. Me in my new suit and Maggie with her dress stretched round her belly. The woman doin the vows seemed a bit snidey and my auntie Jessie said she was a dried up old hoor. Archie and Lizzie signed for us as witnesses and Ah noticed a few glances between them but at the time Ah never paid much attention to it. Ah was too busy gettin married. Then we piled into a coupla motors and went to the Fiveways for the reception.

It was a good do. A few beers and sandwiches and a bit of a bop. Me and Maggie had been practisin this dance for weeks, so we'd put on a good show for the old yins. And they were impressed. Ah saw my auntie Jessie dab her eyes and Maggie's ma was greetin. Then wee Rab got up on the stage and did us a song. He was only six at the time but ye'd have thought he was older. D'ye hear that singin? said my uncle Albert noddin to his pals. That's my fuckin boy.

He stood up and reached his hand to my auntie Jessie. Their fingers linked and didnay part till the clappin and cheerin at the end of the song. Wee Rab ran up sayin was Ah good was Ah good and Albert lifted him by the oxters and held him on his hip. My auntie Jessie put her arm round her men and glowed.

After the dance Ah saw Gambo wanderin around like a lost sheep. What's the matter with ye? Ah said to him. He asked if Ah'd seen Lizzie. Then Maggie asked me if Ah'd seen her coz she wanted to say cheerio before we left for the hotel. So Ah went to look for her. Ah checked the lounge and some of the back rooms and went into the kitchen as a last resort.

She was bent over a table with her bridesmaid's dress halfway up her back and Archie bangin away like he was muggin her. Ah was that shocked Ah just stood there and watched. Then Archie noticed me, so he jammed his cock back into his trousers and pulled Lizzie's dress over her arse. Just as she was smoothin it down, Gambo walked in. The four of us stood there dumb until Archie broke the spell by sayin what the fuck are ye lookin at?

Maggie walked in sayin what's goin on and then she called Archie and Lizzie a pair of dirty bastards. Gambo said that's my girlfriend. Archie looked at Gambo and said what the fuck are ye goin to do about it? Gambo turned and walked out. Ah looked at Archie and shook my head. Ya dirty fucker Ah said, and grabbed Maggie's hand and walked out. We went into the main hall and Jessie asked us what was the matter.

Ah didnay know what to say. Maggie was goin on about her own sister fuckin up her weddin and that was the last she wanted to see of her. Maggie's ma went into the pool room and Ah heard her givin Lizzie a slap. Archie couldnay look my auntie Jessie in the face.

Me and Gambo didnay pal about the gether after that. When Ah got back from the honeymoon Ah found out he'd moved to Hyndland. His ma wouldnay gie me his new address. Yous O'Gradys are nothin but trouble and Ah'm no giein ye the chance to hurt my boy again. Ah couldnay blame her. As for Lizzie, she moved in with Archie and, as Maggie said, she'd made her bed so she could fuckin lie in it.

★

Sean?

Aye.

Have ye spoke to Maggie?

Sean walked to Albert's station.

Fuck sake Albert, Ah thought we'd agreed to keep this to ourselves.

She's yer wife.

Sean banged his forehead with his palm.

Exactly Einstein.

She might be able to help.

How, by hittin Archie with a baseball bat and runnin him out of Glesga?

No, but she's a smart lassie. She might have some good ideas.

It'll worry the fuck out her. She'll think Ah'll be gettin involved in his business to pay it back.

But ye will.

Ah'll probably have to if Ah cannay get some money the gether.

Albert crossed his arms and nodded like an old woman.

Well then.

Maggie doesnay need to know that. Does she? And anyway, it's none of her business. It's between me and Archie.

But she's yer wife.

So?

Well ye should tell her.

D'ye tell my auntie Jessie every detail of your life?

No.

So why are ye tellin me to?

Ah don't want ye to make the same mistakes and

have to learn the same lessons. It's fuckin hard that way.

Sean rammed a chicken onto a hook.

Ah cannay tell her.

How no?

She's a woman. It's my job to look after her, no the other way about.

Albert pointed at Sean.

Stop makin excuses son.

Chickens started landing in Sean's station, so he ran over to sort them out.

Albert joined him at his station.

So are ye goin to tell her?

Ah don't know. What's the point of worryin her?

She'll find out sooner or later.

Ah'd rather it was later.

Albert scratched his head.

Ah don't understand you Sean.

Sean looked Albert in the eye.

She'll hit the fuckin roof.

Albert laughed.

Ah knew ye were feart.

Sean pointed at Albert.

Don't be fuckin cheeky ya cunt.

Albert put his hands up.

Alright wee man. Take it easy.

Ah'm no henpecked, if that's what yer thinkin.

Everybody's a bit scared of their wives.

Sean puffed out his chest.

Ah'm fucked if Ah am.

Ah am.

What, really?

Aye well ye've seen yer auntie Jessie in action.

Sean nodded. Albert went on.

Well if ye think that's bad ye should have seen her when she was younger. My God, what a temper. Many a time she's blew up and started throwin things around the house.

Sean laughed.

Ah can just see my auntie Jessie giein it laldie with a brush in her hand.

Albert pointed at a scar on his forehead.

And d'ye see this?

Ye got that on a buildin site in Bishopbriggs.

No.

So how did ye get it?

Ye cannay be sayin anythin to yer auntie.

Sean crossed himself.

No. Ah swear on it.

We were havin a row one night and she threw a fuckin knife at me. Stuck right in. Ah had to tug the fuckin thing to get it back out.

Sean could hardly believe it.

And ye never hit her back?

No. So have ye ever hit Maggie?

Have Ah fuck. When she blows up Ah just fuck off down the Fiveways till she cools down.

So ye are scared of her.

Sean winked.

Sometimes. But it's no so much that. What really fucks me off is when Ah get the silent treatment. It can go on for days. Ye feel like smashin the house up after a coupla hours, never mind fuckin days.

If ye think she'll be sulkin after ye tell her this, think how long she'll sulk if she finds out from Sammy or some old gossip in the street.

True enough.

Well are ye goin to tell her?

Ah'll think about it.

Albert's station started pumping out chickens, so Sean helped him for a bit. They stood side by side and hung chickens. Then Sean's station started. They looked at each other and smiled. Sean walked over and got to grips with some birds. They dropped in an untidy pile and he knew he'd have to go like fuck to clear them before they ended up on the floor. They weren't very big or heavy though. Cheap birds for small families. Enough for a meal for the four of them with nothing left over for the man's sandwiches on the Monday. In fact it would be a skimpy meal the wife would have to make-up for by doing extra roast potatoes and vegetables. The chicken bones would end up in the bin with all the meat sucked off them. Like they'd been lying on the beach. Even the rats wouldn't bother with them.

Out the corner of his eye he saw Sammy come into the Junction. Sean waited for him to come over and start asking after Archie's money. As the chickens fell, his back tensed with the shadow of Sammy. Sean thought he felt his smelly breath on his neck and he shivered. But the chickens were falling too quick for him to turn and have a word. He could feel Sammy stare right through his jacket and overalls and into his heart. Like he could scan his soul and see wee Donna enjoying the proceeds of Archie's crime. Eventually the chickens slowed and Sean turned to speak but Sammy was up the other side of the Junction talking to Albert.

Sammy was leaning down with his head almost touching Albert's. The old boy had his back to the conveyor belt. He was shaking his head and shrugging his shoulders. Sammy pointed at Sean with his thumb and noticed Sean was looking. He showed Albert the back of his hand before he walked out of the Junction.

Sean went to walk over to Albert but the line started pumping chickens and he had to go back and sort them out. It was cold but he felt a wave of heat hit his cheeks. The chickens built to a fair-sized pile on the belt before he got it together to start hanging them. As he cleared them, he saw the yellow gloved hands of Albert amongst the chickens. The pile receded fast and disappeared. Albert turned to Sean.

That Sammy's a sly fucker.

Tell me somethin Ah don't know.

He'll have ye.

He's no clever enough to have me.

Albert narrowed his eyes.

Ah'm serious son. Ye need to keep yer eye on him.

Ah've always watched Sammy.

Albert took his cap off.

He's tryin to get ye.

What are ye talkin about?

He asked me how ye'd got on down the bank.

And what did ye say?

Ah telt him Ah didnay know what he was talkin about.

Right answer. Then what did he say?

That ye better have got on at the bank or ye were in trouble.

Sean scratched his head.

He's a cheeky bastard so he is.

But he said he'd sort ye out if ye needed it.

Aye Ah know.

But when he said it he was gloatin.

Aye but he would be.

It was more than that Sean. He's got somethin up his sleeve.

Sean was startled out of his worry by chickens landing on his station. He picked them up and hung them without much trouble. The rhythm was easy. Just the right speed to keep his muscles loose and his brain active. If they kept at this pace all day the shift would go past in a flash.

George came into the Junction and told Sean he had a phone call.

Who from?

Yer missus.

What does she want?

She says it's urgent.

Sean dropped a chicken back onto the conveyor belt.

Urgent?

Aye that's what Ah said, urgent.

The foreman squeezed between Sean and the chickens.

Ah'll handle these wee man. Get down the office and take the call from yer wife.

Sean wandered out of the Junction. By the time he was into Fresh he was walking fast. By the time he was in the corridor he was running. He barged into the office and stood by the receptionist's desk.

Ah've got a phone call he gasped.

The receptionist put her finger on the chart she was filling in and looked up at Sean.

Your name?

Sean O'Grady.

The receptionist pointed to a desk in the corner and picked up the phone.

Ah'm puttin you through now Mrs O'Grady.

The phone on the desk started to ring. Sean hurried over and picked it up.

Alright hen?

No.

What is it?

Archie's here.

Sean sat at the desk.

What? Is he in the house?

Aye. He wants to speak to ye.

Sean pulled his cap off.

Put him on.

Ah cannay now, he's went up to the toilet. He's lookin for somethin in the cistern.

Tell him Ah'm on the phone.

Sean heard Maggie shouting up the stairs and Archie come down them.

Sean?

Alright Archie?

Where is it?

There's some of it under the stairs.

How much?

Three hunner.

Where's the fuckin rest of it?

Ah'll no be able to get it till Ah finish work.

Ah want it now.

But Ah cannay gie ye it now.

How the fuck no?

Sean looked around the office until his eyes settled on the receptionist.

It's in the bank.

Oh aye?

Aye. Ah felt a bit paranoid with it all in the house, so Ah thought Ah'd split it.

So ye've no drawn it out then?

No yet. Ah'll get it this afternoon.

Archie laughed a laugh that wasn't funny.

Ye fuckin better.

Sean heard Archie telling Maggie to make him a cup of tea.

Ye've got a lovely lookin wee wife here pal.

The phone went dead. Sean said hello a couple of times but there was nobody there. He shook the phone and said hello again. Then he hung up and tried to phone back. It was engaged. He tried again and it was engaged. He walked to the receptionist's desk and back again. He tried the phone and it was still engaged. He could picture Archie towering over Maggie and asking questions about Sean's money situation. The telephone handset lying on its side on the coffee table. Archie pointing at Maggie saying right where is it? And wee Maggie trying to stand up to him but she'd have a quiver in her voice. And Archie would end up –

Sean swallowed a hard lump of saliva and looked around the bright room. His heart pumped and he felt like being sick. The receptionist looked up and asked him if everything was alright. Sean nodded and tried the phone again. It was still engaged. He tried it again. Still engaged.

He stood by the phone and leaned against the wall. It was roasting in the office. He sucked in a long breath and tried to calm the panic that was making his hands clumsy. Then he picked up the phone and dialled his number. It was still engaged. He slammed it down and the receptionist looked up.

Do you need any help?

Sean looked at her for a second.

No, yer alright.

He thought about picking the phone up again but the receptionist was still looking at him. He mumbled thanks at her and left the office. When he got into the corridor he stopped and pulled his gloves on. Then he pulled them off. He walked to the toilet and rolled a smoke. He stood by the wash basins and looked at his reflection. He watched the lit end of the fag glow as he sucked on the roll-up. He grimaced.

Ye've done it this time kid.

He was in trouble and he knew it. Archie was on one and there was no telling what he'd do when he found out the money was light. Sean spat on the floor and rubbed it into the tiles with the sole of his welly. He walked back and forward as he puffed on his fag. He blew the smoke through his nose as he sucked in more through his mouth. He finished the fag with a triple draw and dropped the end into a urinal. Then he went over to the wash basins and took off his cap. He placed it at the side of a sink. He put on the cold tap and let it run for a while. He cupped his hands under the flow and brought a handful of water to his face.

CHAPTER 10

Sean didn't skip back to the Junction, he dragged his feet through Fresh like they were bags of coal. He walked up to George and grunted. George looked at Sean.

Alright?

Sean grabbed a chicken.

Aye.

George pulled his cap back as he looked at Sean.

Well if there's anythin Ah can do, gie's a shout.

Cheers pal.

George stood for a moment longer, then he left the Junction. Albert came over to Sean's station and patted him on the back.

Everythin alright wee man?

No, is it fuck.

What's the matter?

Ah've just spoke to Archie.

What did he say?

Sean told him. Albert nodded.

So how did he leave it?

He said Ah had a lovely missus then the phone went dead.

Albert's forehead creased.

What d'ye think he meant by that?

Ah'm tryin no to think about it.

They were silent for a bit. Then Albert's eyes lit up.

It could've been a fault with the line. Did ye try to phone back?

Aye but it was engaged.

Albert looked to the floor.

Oh.

Sean felt crushed. Albert reached his hand out and clasped Sean on the shoulder.

He'll probably no do anythin till he's sure the money's gone.

Sean looked his uncle in the eye.

D'ye think?

Albert's hand gripped Sean's shoulder and gave it a little shake.

Course Ah am. He can be a cunt but he's no stupid.

Sean wasn't convinced.

Aye.

Sean's station dropped chickens so he picked them up and hung them. They were only little but they felt heavy. They dropped with their wings tucked into their sides, like welchers protecting their kidneys against violent debt collectors. Sean winced as they bounced on the conveyor belt with a sweaty slap. He picked them up with as much tenderness as he could and placed them on hooks that took them out of sight. But they kept falling. There was never a moment free from the wounded chickens. As soon as he hung one and watched it disappear, one or two would drop onto his station, clutching sides with wings, and sometimes rolling back and forward in agony. He sent hundreds of crippled victims on their way before the last one was dangling on a hook like a prisoner in a mafia film dancing his merry way towards a highly skilled torturer.

George appeared and told Sean and Albert it was time for break. Sean pulled his gloves off and threw them under the conveyor as him and Albert left the Junction for the canteen.

When they got there, the queue stretched all the way to the door and it wasn't moving very fast. Albert got into the queue and Sean went to the phone. He put his last ten pence in the slot and rung his number. It was engaged. He slammed the phone down. A guy was looking at him.

We've all got to use that phone son.

Sean picked the phone up and slammed it back down.

Is it your phone?

The guy looked away.

Sean walked to the canteen queue. He nudged Albert.

It's still fuckin engaged.

We'll try again in a wee while.

The queue was getting cramped. Sean could feel people press against his back. The old fucker in front of him even stood on his toes. He felt like hitting some cunt a punch in the snout. He looked at Albert and the old guy smiled.

Ah think ye need a beer wee man.

What are ye, a mind-reader?

Albert looked at his watch.

We've got twenty minutes.

Time enough.

C'mon then.

They pushed their way out of the queue. Sean turned to Albert.

And anyway we cannay have a private conversation in amongst that crowd of old women.

They walked out of the factory and into the yard. As they got to the gate the security guard gave them a wink and a smile.

Off out are we?

Albert made a drinking motion as he walked. The security guard winked.

Don't come back drunk.

Albert turned round and walked backwards.

Ah'll bring ye back a pint if ye like.

The security guard laughed.

It's more than my life's worth to get caught on the piss.

Ah, well, if yer sure.

Albert made a fag as they walked. He pushed it into his mouth and lit it. After a few puffs he turned to Sean.

He's alright him eh?

He's a fuckin wanker.

Takes one to know one.

Albert took another puff on his fag. He put his arm round Sean's shoulder as they walked.

We'll sort this out son.

Sean rolled a fag, put it in his mouth and lit it. They walked in silence for a while. The pavement narrowed and Sean walked on the road. He looked at Albert and they were the same height. Albert looked at Sean.

Alright wee man?

Sean didn't know whether to laugh or cry. A lorry came down the street so he got on the pavement behind his uncle. He could see little bits of dandruff stuck to his greasy hair. There was the odd grey one but it would be a few years before he could qualify as a Grecian 2000 merchant. The lorry swished past on the brown slush and Sean got back on the road. It was better walking on the road. Less snow to work through. Albert looked at Sean.

Let's hope yer auntie's in.

Aye Ah know.

Ah'm no promisin Ah'll be able to do anythin.

It's good of ye to try.

Have ye any other ideas?

Sean sucked air through his teeth. He hesitated and stuttered.

Ah was thinkin of talkin to Gambo.

Albert nodded wisely.

That's better than nothin.

Thing is with Gambo. He'll want somethin and ye know what that'll mean. If Archie finds out he'll fuckin kill me.

Yer fuckin right he will.

Sean got a whiff of beer and looked up the street. The pub sign swung and the Arab sword blazed as it reflected the sun. Sean put his head down and walked faster. Albert lagged behind. Sean got to the door and pulled it open. He bent like a servant and waved Albert in front of him. Albert dropped his fag and stood on it on the way in. He walked towards the bar.

Go and try the phone. Ah'll get us a drink. Heavy?

Sean nodded.

Have ye got any change?

Albert jingled his pockets and pulled out a handful. Sean picked some ten pences off the pile and went to the phone box in the corridor by the toilets. It rang for ages before Maggie answered. She was panting.

Hello she said.

Maggie, are ye alright?

Aye Ah just ran down the stairs when Ah heard the phone.

What were ye doin up the stairs?

Ah was on the toilet.

Where's Archie?

He's went down to Easterhouse.

Ah didnay think he'd want to see Lizzie.

Aye well that pair are well–suited so they are.

So what was he sayin?

What, after he'd searched my house?

Sean looked at the back of his hand.

Aye.

Aye ya prick. What was that money for?

He asked me to watch it while he was in the jail.

And you said aye?

What was Ah supposed to do?

So how come he was aggravated when he left?

Ah'll tell ye later.

No, ye'll no. Ye can tell me the now.

Sean rolled his eyes.

Ah've no got time. Ah'll tell ye the night.

If ye willnay tell me –

Sean kicked the wall.

Ye'll what?

Ah'll go back to my mammy's. And Ah'll take Donna with me.

Calm down for fuck sake. Yer blowin it out of proportion.

How can Ah calm down when that loony's been stompin all over my house?

The phone was silent for a bit.

What's goin on? said Maggie.

Sean looked at some guy squeezing past then spoke quieter into the phone.

Ah'll tell ye the night.

Ye can tell me now.

Sean's ear felt like it was stuck to the phone. He waited till the guy was out of earshot.

Ah've spent some of Archie's money.

Ye what? How did that happen?

The pips are goin. Ah'll talk to ye when Ah get home.

He cut her off with his finger then put the phone down. He looked up and down the corridor. He straightened himself up and pushed through the corridor door and back into the pub. He walked past the flickering one-armed bandit and under the oak beam. His head was so full of Maggie and Archie he tripped coming down the step and had to run forward to stop himself falling on his face. An old man glanced up from the seat in the corner.

Ye need to watch yer step son.

Thanks for lettin me know.

The old man got back to his paper, his pipe and his

pint. Sean gave him the fingers and stumbled over to the bar.

Sean picked his pint up and wiped the bottom across the towel on the bar. Then he lifted it towards Albert.

Ah fuckin need this.

He had a long swig and smacked his lips like a child. Albert pointed at Sean with his glass.

What's happenin then?

Sean looked at the barman, who walked up to the end of the bar and started polishing glasses.

Maggie's lightened up a bit coz Archie's went to Easterhouse.

Ah didnay think he'd want to go there.

Sean nodded.

Aye well, yer hole's yer hole for all that.

Right enough.

Ah wouldnay want to be in Lizzie's shoes though.

Does he know about the wean?

He'll find out soon enough.

Albert grimaced.

Mind what happened to her the last time?

Sean remembered the guy from Balornock.

Ye should've seen what he did to the guy that fucked her.

Batter him did he?

And the fuckin rest.

Serves the cunt right. It's askin for it, shaggin a guy's missus while he's away in the jail.

Aye and her gettin pregnant this time. When he goes round there he'll see the evidence. It's only a matter of time before –

Albert had a swallow and wiped his mouth with the back of his hand.

Ouch.

Sean took a swig.

Best of it is she thinks he might take her and the wean on.

Albert shook his head.

Will she ever learn?

Aye Ah know. She was last in the queue when God was dishin out brains.

Just think. If she had a bit more sense she could've been with yer mate Gambo. Livin up the West End. Nice wee motor. Holidays abroad.

Bit different from a two-bedroom flat in Easterhouse. Albert laughed.

Aye no half.

They stared at their pints for a few seconds, then Albert looked at his watch.

Right. Ah'd better go and phone yer auntie Jessie. Sean took his pint over to a corner table next to the window. He sat down and put his beer on a mat. He grabbed another mat and picked at its soggy edges. When he'd made a little pile of torn cardboard, he got his tobacco out. He had the fag rolled and was licking the paper when Albert appeared from the phone.

So?

Aye.

Aye?

That's what Ah said.

How much?

Five hunner.

Sean picked up his pint and knocked it against Albert's.

That's fuckin –

Don't get too excited, she's got some conditions.

Sean tried to look adult.

What are they?

She wants ye to pay the money back on a week by week basis.

No problem. Every time Ah pick up my wages, Ah'll gie ye what ye want towards the loan.

Twenty pound.

Sean looked out the window then back to Albert.

OK. Twenty pound every Friday.

Sean leaned back in his seat and sparked his fag. Albert had another swig on his beer.

There's more.

Sean sat forward. He tried to look serious.

Oh aye?

She wants ye to tell Maggie.

Sean nodded.

Ah just telt her.

What did she say?

Nothin really. Ah mean, what could she say?

Albert wiped his mouth.

Doesnay sound like Maggie to me.

Sean laughed.

Aye well, we'll no doubt have a few words when Ah get in from work.

Albert frowned and cleared his throat.

It's good ye've telt her son, coz it's always better to be honest with yer wife.

Sean picked at the bits of beer mat.

Ah know.

She'll maybe shout and scream for a coupla days but when the dust settles she'll respect ye for facin her and tellin the truth.

Sean had a swallow of his pint. He felt a bit awkward.

So when can Ah get the money?

Alright son, Ah'll shut up now.

They laughed.

We can call into the bank on the way back to work.

Will they gie ye it just like that?

It's my fuckin money.

Aye right enough.

Albert stood up.

Right c'mon then.

Sean swallowed the rest of his pint and stood up. He picked up the empty glasses and put them on the bar on their way out.

As they walked down the street the cold hit him so he zipped up his jacket.

It's fuckin freezin.

Albert zipped up his jacket and pulled his cap firmer onto his head.

Ye can say that again wee man.

Sean elbowed Albert.

Colder than a hoor's legs.

Albert laughed.

Trust you to lower the tone.

Sean laughed.

Colder than the foreman's wife.

Albert never said anything so Sean shut up. He got his

tobacco out and made a roll-up. As he smoked, he had a look at the town. It was not a bad wee place. One day, if him and Maggie ever got the money together, he'd like to move from Royston and buy a bungalow in a town like this. A man could have a good life here. He could get up about ten for a late breakfast. Some coffee and a couple of slices of toast and marmalade. Then put the clothes on and have a wander up the town. Maybe call into the butcher's for a half pound of sausages for dinner. Get some potatoes and a paper. Call into the pub for a pint. Put a couple of lines on at the bookie's. Then wander home and have some sausages and mash, a couple of cans of beer, and a lazy afternoon seeing how the horses done on Channel Four racing. Lovely.

They walked down the tree-lined street until they came to the arcade. Sean touched Albert on the arm. They stopped on the pavement.

Shall Ah wait here for ye?

Ye can come in if ye want.

Sean looked at the bank and remembered the old dear.

No. Ah couldnay face that again the day.

Albert called over his shoulder as he stepped off the pavement.

Fair enough wee man.

Sean ducked under the arcade and rolled himself another fag. He leaned on a pillar and felt the cold and the smoke beat up his lungs.

*

Ah got a phone call from my uncle Albert one Monday afternoon. My auntie Jessie had took a heart attack and was in the Royal Infirmary. Ah got washed and changed and got the first bus into the city centre. Ah was fucked if Ah was missin out on another relative. When Ah got there, Albert was sat at the side of the bed with her hand in his and she was sleepin. There was pipes goin in and out of her and a machine beeped away at the side of the bed.

Ah drew up a chair and sat on it with my flowers in my lap. Ah didnay know what else to do. Eventually a nurse came up and took the flowers out my hand and put them in a vase. Ah followed her into the station and asked what the score was with my auntie. The nurse telt me she should be alright. They'd caught her in plenty of time. With a bit of care in the hospital, and a change of diet when she got home, there was no reason why she couldnay live for a few years to come.

Ah went back to the bedside and clapped my uncle on the back. Is there anythin Ah can do? He gave me the same look he gave my auntie when he telt us our mammy was dead. Poor old bastard. It was like he didnay know where he was. So Ah asked him about Rab and he started, coz he'd forgotten all about the boy. Ah telt him Ah'd get down the school and pick him up.

Rab came back to our house and Maggie made him his dinner. Ah said Ah'd take him up the hospital. Maggie shook her head but Ah remember how Ah felt when no cunt took me to see my mammy so Ah thought fuck it and took him up there. When Albert saw me walk into the ward with Rab he got the huff, but the boy was old enough to cope with an hour watchin his mammy have a wee sleep.

Ah went to see my auntie Jessie every night when she was in the hospital. Our Archie went up once and dropped a bunch of roses off and spent a half-hour lookin at his watch. My uncle was a bit pissed off with him. Archie's got a fuckin motor so there's no reason why he couldnay make an effort and get up there through the day. It's no as if the cunt's got a job.

But as Archie said, hospitals gave him the heebie-jeebies. And no wonder when yer ma went into one of the places and never came out.

When my auntie was better, Ah went round to see her. She gave me a cuddle and pushed a twenty-pound note into my hand. Ah didnay want to take it but she wouldnay let me leave without it. Said she knew Ah was short and with all the bus fares to and from the hospital Ah must be about skint. No to mention the amount of grub wee Rab can eat. She telt me she'd never forget what Ah'd done and Ah'd shown the difference between me and my brother. Ah telt her no to worry about it. If it wasnay for her and my uncle, me and Archie would've ended up in a home. And fuck that for a game of soldiers.

★

Sean didn't have to wait very long before Albert came out of the bank and passed him a brown envelope. He tried to take it but Albert gripped it between his thumb and forefinger. He looked Sean in the eye.

Remember the conditions.

Sean nodded and tried to look serious.

Ah remember.

Albert nodded and let the envelope go. Sean tucked it into the inside pocket of his jacket. He wanted to count it but thought Albert might get angry if he did it in front of him. It would be best to leave that part till he was on his own in the toilets.

Sean and Albert walked back to the factory. Sean was buzzing. He walked erect and his chest was taking deep breaths of the lovely air. They soon reached the factory gates and, as they entered, the security guard looked at his watch.

What time d'ye call this?

Sean looked and smiled.

Fuck off company man.

The security guard winked at Sean and looked at Albert.

Where's my pint then?

Albert pointed behind him with his thumb.

It's in the Saracen.

The security guard laughed.

Ah'll pick it up after work.

No problem. What time d'ye make it?

The security guard looked at his watch.

Twenty to one.

Albert looked at his watch.

Ah make it half twelve.

The security guard looked at his watch

Come to think of it, my watch is a bit fast. Half twelve sounds about right.

Albert winked at him.

Ah thought so.

Sean and Albert walked into the yard. Sean screwed up his face.

Would ye smell that?

Aye Ah know, it's fuckin bowfin.

They got to the factory door and Sean ran ahead.

Last one in's an Englishman.

They bumped into Sammy in the corridor. He was coming towards the canteen from Fresh.

Where were ye? Ah've just been up Fresh lookin for ye.

Sean looked at Albert then back at Sammy.

In the canteen.

Aye, my arse. Ah can smell the drink from here.

Albert mumbled.

Better than the smell of shite.

Sammy looked at Albert.

What was that?

Ah said beer improves the sight.

Sammy looked confused, shook his head and turned to Sean.

Can Ah have a word?

Aye go ahead said Sean.

Sammy nodded at Albert.

In private said Sammy.

Sean looked at Albert, who nodded and walked towards Fresh.

Ah'll keep an eye on yer line till ye get back. Don't be long.

Sammy gave Albert's back the fingers.

Miserable old bastard.

Sean pointed at Sammy.

Mind he's my uncle.

Aye whatever. C'mon.

Sammy led Sean to the toilets. When they were in there, Sammy had a good look about.

Walls have ears.

Sean laughed.

Ye've watched too many spy films.

Ah'm fuckin serious, ye cannay be too careful who knows yer business. Knowledge is power and that.

Aye alright big man. What d'ye want?

Sammy pointed to the door.

Just put yer foot against that door.

He pulled a packet out of his pocket and tapped some powder onto the edge of a wash basin. He made a rough line and bent down to snort it.

Yer comin the cunt now.

Sammy stood up sniffling and rubbing his nose. He nodded towards the wash basin.

D'ye want a line?

Sean looked left and right. He licked his lips.

No, Ah better no.

Sammy shrugged.

Suit yerself.

He sorted another line on the basin then bent down for a sniff. He shook his head and sniffed a big mouthful of snot down his throat.

Cheers for holdin the door pal.

Sean smiled.

No bother son. That'll make the rest of the day go whizzin past.

Sammy laughed at the joke and got his tobacco out.

Here, d'ye want a fag?

He pulled out his pouch and passed it to Sean. Then he wiped the basin with his finger and gave it a good suck. When Sean had rolled a fag, he passed the tobacco back. Sammy grabbed it and rolled himself a fag. Every few seconds he gave Sean a look as if he was about to ask something. Then he asked.

Can ye play brag?

Course Ah can.

D'ye want a game?

Sean gave his lips another lick.

Who with?

Coupla guys from Packin. They've got plenty of money.

Oh aye?

Sammy rubbed his fingers against his thumb and nodded.

It's payday wee man.

Sean felt his back pocket.

So, when's the game?

One o'clock.

What about my work?

Get yer uncle to look after it.

What about the foreman?

Don't worry about that cunt. Ah'll gie him a tenner

if he shows his face. Or Ah'll offer him a batterin. That'll shut him up.

So where's the game?

Come down to Frozen just before one o'clock and Ah'll take ye to it.

CHAPTER 11

Sean walked to his station and bent down to get his gloves from under the conveyor belt. He pulled them on and waited for the chickens. It wasn't long and one appeared over the horizon. He felt like a hitchhiker in Texas or somewhere. It was getting on and he hadn't had a lift all morning. The sun was beating down on his poor wee head and his lips were chapped. His tongue stuck to the roof of his mouth. Then, a long way away on this American road straight out the films, a car appeared. It got closer and closer. The dust trail was massive. His whole life zoned in on this possible carriage out of the hell of the American countryside. It drew up beside him, the door opened with a hiss and it fell onto his conveyor belt with a slap. He picked it up and hung it on a hook.

Then came a bit of a traffic jam. Loads of them appeared. One after the other. Sean prepared himself for the onslaught by cricking his fingers and looking over to Albert. They nodded at each other. Chickens were everywhere, and Sean had barely enough time to workout how he was going to get away from the Junction for a game of cards. Not that it mattered. If he hung on to the money he had, he'd just be two hundred under what Archie gave him. Not too bad.

He couldnay complain about that.

But he would. He'd want to know how come the money went missing. He'd use it against Sean at every turn. Sean would have to run some drugs about to pay the money back. Just not as much as if he'd lost the lot. If Sean could make up the losses, he could go about his business without the threat of a late-night visit. Last thing he needed was to be woke up at midnight and asked to drive a car to Edinburgh or London or Possil.

Aye there was no point in just having the eight hundred. Might as well have nothing. Archie was going to be angry unless he had the lot. The best thing to do would be to go to the cards with two hundred as a limit, and if it dropped more than that to stop playing and come straight back to the Junction. All it would take would be a bit of self-discipline. He might even walk out of Frozen with Archie's money and a few quid for spends anyway. That would be excellent. Give Archie his cash and then take Maggie out for a well-deserved dinner. Table for two and a wee drop of bubbly. Waiter pulling the seat out as she goes to sit down. She'd love that. Sean would get the lord and master treatment for weeks after. Woken up by a gammy on Sunday morning followed by breakfast in bed.

Lovely.

Thing to do now was come up with a wee scheme that would let Sean out of the Junction for a while and not tell Albert that he was playing cards with the boys from Packing. He could try the dodgy belly routine. Go to the toilets and kid on he'd been there for an hour. But that wouldn't work. Albert would tell him he'd made a quick recovery. Especially if he won. But then again, if he won he wouldn't care what Albert thought. He could just give him his money back.

Ah'll tell him.

Albert was right behind Sean.

Tell who what?

Sean nearly shat himself.

What are ye doin sneakin up on me? Could've gave me a fuckin heart attack.

Alright wee man, take it easy.

Sorry. It's just ye gave me a bit of a fright.

Yer jumpy the day.

Can ye fuckin blame me?

Albert's eyes brightened up and he nodded.

Aye Ah can.

What d'ye mean aye?

Ye've got yerself into a sorry state so ye have.

What?

Yer no entirely blameless. Are ye?

Ye don't know how temptin it is to have all that money lyin about the house.

Just coz yer tempted to do somethin doesnay mean ye have to do it.

What are ye, a fuckin saint?

Ah've had my problems.

Ye wouldnay fuckin think so, the way yer goin on.

Ah never stole off my fuckin brother. Ah know that.

Ah was goin to put it back.

Trouble is, things don't always workout like that.

Ah fuckin know.

Albert's station dropped a couple of chickens. So he walked off. Sean watched his old back for a minute and then his own line popped, so he turned and watched a lonely chicken travelling up the conveyor belt.

Sean felt like a child who's just captured a blue-bottle. The sort of child that doesn't just squash it. First he shakes it in his hands for a bit to stun it. Then he pulls its wings off and calls it a miniature elephant. Roll up, roll up, ladies and gentlemen, boys and girls, welcome to the world famous O'Grady circus and the fabulantastical miniaturalittle elephants. But that wouldn't be right would it? Elephants have four legs and bluebottles have six so he'd have to pull two of its legs off. Preferably the middle legs. When he's fed up with the elephant he pulls off its two back legs. Ladies and gentlemen, it's a beautiful sunny afternoon here in Daytona and I'm glad you could join us for the thirty-third international drag racing champion-ship. It's a bit of an anti-climax after Daytona. He pulls its last two legs off, watches it meditate for a while. Then he squashes it.

Sean sent the broken chicken on its way and tried to work up to having a sore belly. He grabbed it and went aaah, but could feel a blush coming on, so the chances of pulling it off in front of his uncle were slim. Maybe if he just said he needed a shite he could get off and think up an excuse on the way back. He walked over to Albert's station.

Uncle Albert?

What is it?

Ah'm sorry for snappin at ye.

Albert bit his lip.

Ah know yer under a bit of pressure. Let's just forget about it eh?

Aye OK. Is it alright if Ah nip off for a bit?

Albert turned round with a frown on his forehead.

How? Where are ye goin?

Sean held his belly.

Ah think Ah had a bad pint coz Ah'm dyin for a shite.

Albert's frown eased.

Aye go on then son.

Sean's heart pounded as he walked down the steps and into Fresh. The fluorescent lights were dazzling and he could make out the slight flicker in the one closest to the corridor. He pushed through the plastic door and the walk to the toilet seemed like a hundred miles. He went straight to a cubicle, locked himself in and drew the envelope full of money out of his pocket. He tore the side off and slid out the wedge of tenners. A quick count and there was forty-nine of them.

Forty-nine? That's no right.

He banged the wedge against his hand and recounted it. Fifty, right enough.

Fuckin eejit, ye cannay even count, never mind play cards.

He tucked the cash into his pocket. He crushed the envelope, dropped it into the bowl and pulled the chain. It danced around in the water and he thought it wasn't going to flush away, but at the last moment it caught the current and whipped round the U-bend. All that remained was a small triangle of brown paper circling round a dying whirlpool.

He looked at the water for a bit then he got up and opened the door, went to the sink and washed his hands. He caught his eye in the mirror and almost flinched.

C'mon wee man. Ye can do this.

His mirror image looked up and they stared into each other's eyes like lovers, or men about to fight.

No bother.

He left the toilet and walked with his head down. He heard the odd Sean crackling through the air as he passed people he knew. He nodded in reply but didn't stop to chat. Before long he was pushing his way into Frozen.

The cold hit his lungs like a dry cigarette. He breathed shallow and headed towards a golden light. As he drew near he could make out the window in a steel cubicle that was putting out the rays. He opened the door and walked into the cubicle. There was a guy in there hunched over a computer.

Where's Sammy? said Sean.

He'll be back in a minute.

Sean rubbed his hands together.

It's cold in here.

The guy turned his screwed-up face towards Sean.

That's coz cunts keep openin the fuckin door.

Oh sorry.

The guy hunched back over his terminal and mumbled.

Three tons of chicken wings for Doncaster. How the fuck do they expect us to have that ready for the morra?

The door opened and Sammy looked in. He flicked his head at Sean, who followed him out of the hut. Sammy nodded to the hut.

Ye didnay say anythin to that cunt did ye?

Did Ah fuck.

Good coz the stupid prick always wants a game but he's never got any money. Starts fuckin about with ten-bob raises. We're playin for bigger money than that.

Sean felt the pulse jump through his throat at the sound of the big money.

That's what Ah'm here for.

Sammy touched Sean on the shoulder.

One thing though pal. There's no skinflints or tick merchants on our game, so gie's a look at yer stake.

D'ye no trust me?

Ye know me son. Ah trust no cunt.

Sean pulled his wedge out his overalls and gave Sammy a quick swatch.

Good enough for ye?

Sammy gave Sean a frown.

Aye that'll do. Sorry wee man, it's just that Ah cannay be lettin ye get into trouble because ye've no enough to cover the stakes. C'mon.

Sammy walked through the Frozen wastes and out the door into the corridor. Sean followed, watching Sammy's key chain jangling like a jailer's.

Where are we goin?

Sammy looked over his shoulder.

Ye'll find out when we get there.

He pushed through an emergency door and held it open for Sean.

Push it back till it looks shut but doesnay click. We might need to get back this way.

They walked between a barbed-wire fence and the factory wall for a hundred yards. An electricity substation hummed as they squeezed between it and the fence. Sean pulled bits of leaves and spiders' webs out of his hair.

Fuck sake Sammy, where are we?

Sammy put a finger to his lips.

Shh.

He pointed to an open space ahead. There was a guy in a suit pacing up and down. He walked with a funny little skip like a wee lassie in the playground. He was having a fag. They would have to wait until he had his smoke and fucked off back into the office. Sean leaned against the substation and looked at the sky. The clouds were grey and it looked like it might snow again.

*

Me and Albert went to the Fiveways one Saturday mornin. It was a lovely day and we got there at eleven. The usual crew were in the bar so we had a coupla pints and a game of pool. Ah didnay pay much attention when one of the boys went on about this sure thing for the gee gees. Said he'd heard about it from some cousin of his that worked as a stable-boy in Newmarket. Thing is the guy that was spreadin the rumour about the horse was always tryin to tap me up for the price of a pint. It made me wonder if he'd really know a sure thing if it hit him on the face. And anyway, a successful gambler's no goin to let every cunt know about his bets. That would be stupid, coz the more money that goes on a horse the shorter the odds.

We left the pub after a few beers and headed home for our dinners. On the way Albert kept goin on about this sure thing. It was soundin more attractive by the minute. He said Ah should gie it a wee try. At ten to one it was well worth a fiver's risk. He couldnay wait to see the look on the bookie's face when he walked out with fifty-five quid. Imagine it son. Fifty-five quid to spend on what ye like coz the wife doesnay know fuck-all about it. He looked like a wee boy when he was tellin me that.

Ah let him blabber on about the horse. Angel's Delight it was called. He said it was a message from God. Ah said it was called Angel's Delight coz it was a fuckin puddin. But Ah went into the bookie's with him anyway and watched him put the bet on. When we'd left and walked about a hunner yards up the street Ah said fuck it, Ah'll have a wee punt and ran back. Ah telt Albert to walk on and Ah'd catch him up.

The truth of the matter was Ah couldnay let him know how much Ah was puttin on. Ah had fifty bar of Archie's money in my pocket. He'd dropped it round the night before and asked me to look after it till

Monday. Ah didnay want to leave it in the house in case Maggie found it and thought Ah was holdin out on her, so Ah kept it in my pocket. It must have been the drink that gave me the bravery to risk it on a horse. Especially one tipped by some old tramp in the local waterin hole. Ah wouldnay have done it sober that's for sure.

As soon as the bookie took my money Ah knew Ah'd made a mistake and asked him for it back, but he just pointed to a sign that said somethin about null and void and no monies are refundable.

Ah caught up with Albert and whined at him. We've made a mistake and Maggie'll kill me. He grabbed me by the shoulder and said c'mon son it's only a wee bit of fun. What's the odd fiver eh? Ye'll soon spend that on the drink. Ah said right enough, and we went up to his house to watch the race on the telly. Ah couldnay believe it when the bastard won. It took a few minutes for the effect to kick in. Then Ah knew Ah was pure fuckin rich. Ah telt my uncle Ah'd run down to the bookie's and pick up our winnins. Ye should've seen the bookie's face. He was gutted. Wished he'd gave me my money back, so he did.

That night Ah asked my auntie Jessie to babysit Donna so that Ah could take Maggie up the toon for a night out. Maggie loved it. She said the best thing about goin out is no havin to wash the dishes after yer dinner. She wanted to know how Ah could afford it. When Ah telt her Ah'd won at the bookie's, she didnay know whether to gie me a cuddle or gie me a row. Ah didnay tell her Ah'd risked fifty bar of Archie's money. She would've went daft. Ah telt her it was one of them Yankee bets where ye put on a coupla pound and the odds are that long if ye win anythin yer laughin. And anyway, Ah only telt her Ah'd won two hunner.

As for the old bookie, he shouldnay have been so miserable coz within a few weeks Ah'd gave him most of his money back. Ah was in there just about every day. Ah started gettin the Racin Post and studyin the form. Ah got so Ah could hardly think of anythin else but the fuckin gee gees. My next mistake was to ask him if Ah could have an account. He rubbed his hands the gether at that. And no fuckin wonder. It gave him a start on my wages before Ah'd even earned them.

After six months Ah owed him a fortune and Ah thought fuck this and started to put my bets on at a bookie's up in Springburn. Ah got an account with him as well but ye cannay keep secrets in the gamblin world. Before Ah knew what was happenin, the first one heard about it and the two of them got the gether and made sure Ah was barred out all the local bettin salons. Then they sold the debts to some shady bastards who werenay feart to bang round the door at all hours tryin to get their money back. And as for the interest. That was unreal.

Maggie was disgusted with me when she found out. She tipped my dinner onto the kitchen floor and stormed off into the living room. She didnay talk to me for three days. But the last straw was when she came home one night and Ah'd took the telly down the pawn for the Derby. She had her bags packed in fifteen minutes. Wee Donna was screamin that she didnay want to go but Maggie dragged her out the house and up to her ma's.

Archie heard about Maggie leavin me from my auntie Jessie. He came round and the house was a shitehole. Chip wrappers and beer cans all over the floor and me lyin on the couch with my face in my hands. He called me all the lazy bastards and gave me a slap round the ear. Made me get a bath and telt me we were goin out. He took me to this house in Springburn, where the debt collectors lived. Turned out he'd met one of them in Barlinnie. The guy didnay want to accept Archie's offer of lettin me off with the money. What would all his other debtors do if they knew he'd let me off? No cunt would pay up would they? Archie nodded and said he could see his point. What are we goin to do then? Archie said they could gie me a batterin and call it quits at that.

They were talkin away as if Ah wasnay there. Ah shat myself, but what else could Ah do? Archie left the house and said he'd be back in a half-hour. The two guys smiled like fuckin sharks and went about me with punches and kicks till Ah was curled up on the floor. When Ah held my head, they kicked me on the back and guts. When Ah tried to protect my guts, they kicked me in the head. Ah thought it was never goin to end. But it did.

The two guys sat down and ye could see the sweat on their faces. Nothin like a bit of exercise one of them said. The other one laughed. Ah felt like greetin.

Archie came in and said thanks to the guys. They said any time big man. Archie helped me up and wiped the blood off my face and Ah hobbled down to the motor. On the way home he said Ah needed to remember there was always consequences to our actions. He could've got me off without a batterin but with lessons like that Ah'd never learn from my mistakes. He asked me if Ah understood what he was goin on about. Ah nodded. Ah couldnay say much coz my gub was killin me. He took me home and made me a cup of tea. He left me to drink it while he went round for Maggie to tell her what happened. Well he gave her the edited highlights.

It didnay turn out too bad though. Archie was good enough to get the telly out the pawn. The batterin gave Maggie enough sympathy to come home. Ah only needed to visit the dentist three times to get my teeth fixed. And as for the broken nose, my auntie Jessie said it gies a guy character.

★

Eventually the guy in the suit had a last puff and blew the smoke into the air. He dropped his fag and stood on it. He was walking to the door when he noticed something on his trouser leg. He brushed it with his hand and scraped it with his fingernail. He spat on his thumb and rubbed it in the spot. He pinched the material to have another look. Then he flicked it with the back of his hand, straightened up and walked through the door back into the office. Sammy nodded his head to Sean and they passed by the door and into another channel between the wall and the fence. They came to another clearing that had a shed in the middle of it. There was steam coming out of a vent in the roof.

Sean looked through the barbed-wire fence and stopped walking. Sammy turned round.

Are ye comin then?

Sean shook his head.

Ah don't know about this Sammy.

What's the matter with ye? Are ye bottlin out?

No it's no that.

Sammy walked towards the hut.

Well come on then. It's only a game of cards for fuck sake.

Sean stuttered.

Ah'm no goin to do it. Fuck this, Ah'm goin back. Sean turned round and started walkin. Sammy ran forward and blocked his way.

But Ah've set this up for ye.

Sorry Sammy but Ah've –

Sammy snarled.

Ye've what?

Sean pushed against him.

Ah've got to get back.

Sammy grabbed him by the overalls and pulled him close.

What d'ye think yer doin, fuckin me about?

Ah'm no. Ah didnay mean to. Ah've just changed my mind.

Sammy shook Sean.

Where's Archie's fuckin money?

Sean struggled free.

That's between him and me.

Sammy pushed him against the wire fence.

He asked me to collect it, so hand it over.

No.

Sammy punched him in the side of the rib cage.

Fuckin hand it over.

Sean ran his head into Sammy and pushed him against the wall. They struggled with each other but Sammy was the better fighter. Sean fell to his knees and tried to hang onto Sammy's overalls. But he was pushed to the ground. Sammy kneeled on his chest and leaned into his face.

Gie's the fuckin money.

He ground his knee into Sean's sternum. Then he let the pressure off. Sean reached into his pocket and pulled the money out. Sammy grabbed it and counted it.

Five hunner? Where's the rest of it?

Sean couldnay say anything. He just rubbed his chest. Sammy got up and gave him a kick on the thigh.

Ye better have it for the night or yer in for it.

He spat on the ground and walked towards the hut.

Sean felt the pain as he stood up. He looked to the floor and saw his cap there, upside down. He bent down and picked it up and put it on. It was getting on for one o'clock. An hour before the factory closed and he had to go home for more slaps. He turned to face the woods.

Jesus fuckin Christ.

He gripped the rusty wire and leaned into the fence and kicked little crescents into the earth with the toes of his wellies. He could soon climb over and live in there and have nobody bothering him. It would be easy enough to set up a camp with branches leaning over a tree-trunk. Maybe get some plastic bags on top to make it waterproof. Live off the land on roots and berries. Set some snares for rabbits. Have a wee fire for the cold nights. Totally independent. He'd just come out once a fortnight to pick up the giro and buy supplies.

He straightened up and started walking. His thigh was sore but was eased by the walk. It didn't take long to get to the fire exit. He went through and clicked the door closed behind him. He looked up and down the corridor and started limping towards the Junction. He rubbed his thigh as he walked. Somebody shouted behind him. He turned round and George was approaching him.

What are you doin away from yer line?

Ah just went to the toilet.

Well ye should have got somebody to cover for ye.

Ah've got Albert doin it.

George looked at him closely.

Are ye alright?

Sean had to watch what he said in case he started crying.

Ah've fucked up big man.

How, what've ye done?

Ah need some money.

One of George's eyebrows went up.

Oh aye?

Sean fiddled with a button on the front of his over-alls.

Ah owe our Archie two hunner pound and Ah need to gie him it the day.

George tutted and gave out a loud sigh.

Ah wish Ah could help ye out son but Ah've got a family to feed.

Sean went to walk back to the Junction.

Fair enough. Ah better get back to work.

George grabbed his arm.

Have ye tried the Credit Union?

Sean felt the factory lighten up a bit.

No.

C'mon to the office. They've got applications there.

It didn't take them long to walk to the office. The receptionist was typing into a computer. George put his clipboard on the counter.

Alright doll?

She took her eyes off the screen. George leaned over the counter.

Gie's a loan application.

She reached under her desk and pulled out a sheet of paper. George grabbed it and signed a dotted line at the bottom.

Ah've gave ye a reference. Don't be asking for a million.

Thanks George.

Right. Get that filled in and Ah'll go and check that Albert's alright.

Sean picked it up and turned to the receptionist.

Have ye got a pen?

She gave him one and he sat by the desk and filled it in. Then he went to the counter and handed the application to her. She took it and put it in a tray. Sean stood by the desk. After she had typed in a few more words on the computer, she turned to him.

Is there anything else?

Ah'm just waitin for my money.

She laughed.

Impatient aren't you? If you're going to get it, you'll get a cheque at the end of the day.

A cheque? Can Ah no get cash?

She wrote something at the bottom of the form.

Come to the office at two o'clock.

Sean winked at her.

What if Ah cannay wait that long?

She laughed and looked at her watch.

Call in at two. You've not got long to wait.

Sean left the office and pushed back into the factory corridor. He wasn't limping anymore. He strode back to Fresh in time to the building rhythm of the poultry moving through the factory. He became worried about Albert and George's ability to cope so he walked faster. Left right left right left right.

The glorious men of the Royston Rifles marched to relieve the Junction. It was a magnificent sight. Dust trailed for miles behind them into a gigantic triangle high in the blue sky. They passed smoking artillery with dead men strewn all around. A vulture picked at a soldier's eyes, its claws curled deep in his chest and its wings unfurled ready to fly at the smoke from a gun. They passed villages of broken children being fed on by clouds of flies. They marched past the tiredness and the hunger and the horror. Most regiments would have rested but not the Royston Rifles. They were disciplined. The men in skirts are brave, they don't eat a lot, and they're fuckin good shots.

He jumped up the stairs and into the Junction. Albert was struggling but he was clearing the chickens from his line. Sean tapped George's shoulder, said cheers mate, and attacked the birds that were falling on his conveyor belt. His timing was brilliant. The factory was reaching its crescendo. Waves of dead birds were attacking his station like suicidal maniacs. Their dead were piling up in front of his guns. Sean moved with calm efficiency and began to extricate legs from the general scrum. As his right hand hung a chicken on a hook, his left hand was searching out another prominent limb. Meanwhile the machine was trying to distract him with a rapid fire of falling chickens. A lesser man would have given up, thrown his gloves at George, and walked into the desert. Not Sean though. He was made of sterner stuff. The likes of him had fought their way out of worse scrapes than this. They had faced down overwhelming odds with nothing but grim determination and sharp bayonets.

Sir, sir.

Yes Dogby.

The chickens are coming sir.

I know Dogby, help me on with my tunic, there's a good chap.

But they're closing in Sir. Undreds of em.

Discipline Dogby, one always has to have discipline. Otherwise one is no better than those damn chickens. Don't worry old chap. God will smile on us this day.

Yes sir.

We will prevail. Hand me my pistol, there's a good chap.

Sir.

Thanks Dogby. Now get your rifle and show me to the chickens. Where's Sergeant O'Grady?

On the fire-step sir.

O'Grady don't shoot until you see the goose bumps on their flesh.

You heard the officer, hold your fire till I give the order.

The Royston Rifles formed a square to defend against the chickens. The ululating heathen disconcerted the men but Sergeant O'Grady ensured discipline was maintained. The enemy erupted from the mountains in a flurry of rifle smoke and orange silk. Their swords curved towards the brave Scottish men. The pounding of their powerful wings became deafening. Sergeant O'Grady told his men to fix bayonets. He waited until the enemy reached the fifty-yard marker and he told his men to fire. They fired. He told his men to load. They loaded. One more volley and the chickens were inside the square. Sergeant O'Grady attacked them like they were bags of straw hung from branches. His rifle soon became sticky with blood. He slipped on the entrails of a screaming soldier. He stabbed and hacked and clubbed and kicked. Smoke and vultures circled overhead.

Sean's rhythm built from back-twinging jerks to a blurred vision of hands working without being told what to do. He felt his biceps loosen then a low heat took hold that increased till he felt a flush of itchiness break out across his back. Then, just as he thought the chickens might defeat him, they slowed, and he felt relief was at hand. He was clearing the pile faster than it was being added to. The chickens stopped falling. The conveyor belt was cleared. Sean pushed his hands into his back and stretched. He exhaled in a noisy breath that rose to the ceiling in a smoke-like plume.

CHAPTER 12

Albert hung his last chicken, walked over to the corner and picked up a brush.

Ah suppose we better gie this place a clean.

Sean grabbed a brush. They started with the conveyor belt. Giving it a sweep and trying to knock all the bits of fat caught in the framework onto the floor. Albert nudged Sean.

Check that poor wee bastard.

Sean looked down into Fresh and there was a white cap struggling with the last of the chickens. Sean picked up a bit of fat and turned to Albert.

Watch this.

He threw the fat at the white cap. It hit him right on the back. The white cap looked up and around, but Sean and Albert were busy cleaning. Sean waited for a minute then flicked another piece of fat. The white cap looked round quicker, but his line dropped some chickens and he had to hang them on the rack. Sean rubbed his hands together and hunted around for more fat. He found a big piece under the conveyor belt and threw it at the white cap. Bang on the back and the white cap started round while chickens pumped off into his station. He realised too late that he was overloaded and had to call George to help him. Sean and Albert shook their heads like disappointed fathers. They got back to the cleaning.

After the framework was done, they swept the floor. Sean came up against a stubborn bit of fat. A couple of stiff strokes and it came loose. He brushed it towards a pile they had gathered next to the bin. He went to the corner and placed his broom against the wall. He got the shovel and scooped up the fat and dumped it in the bin. Albert swept the disordered bits of fat back into a mound. When there wasn't much left, Sean put the shovel in front of the pile and Albert pushed the fat onto it with the brush. Sean dumped this last load into the bin, threw the shovel clanging into the corner and clapped his hands together.

Aye that'll do.

Albert went to the corner and propped the shovel up. He placed the brush beside it.

Take the bin out son.

Sean picked the bin up and slung it onto his shoulder. He walked out of the Junction and into Fresh. The girls in there were all happy at the thought of a weekend with wages to spend. He walked through them to the skip in the corner. He could see all their mouths opening but it was hard to connect the sounds with the mouths. It reminded him of a wildlife documentary about sea lions.

He dumped the binload into the skip. He thought about telling his uncle about the cards as he climbed the steps back into the Junction, but there was no point. It would only cause more grief and there was enough of that to go around already. He walked up to the old boy and both of them leaned against a conveyor belt. Albert took his gloves off.

Aye. Another week over. Ah'll be glad when Ah'm home and bathed.

Ye can say that again.

Then Ah'll be down the Fiveways for a beer.

Sean smacked his lips.

Ah wish Ah could join ye.

Never mind son. Ye'll be out there with the best of us soon enough.

Albert pointed into Fresh.

There he is.

Sean looked and George was wandering through. He had a clipboard and a pile of envelopes. He stopped and talked to an old woman. She was bowing away to him as if he was Prince Charles in to do a factory inspection. He walked away from her and headed for the Junction. Sean tutted.

About fuckin time.

George climbed the stairs and came over with their payslips. Sean tucked his into his overalls.

Cheers big man.

George gave Albert his and turned back to Sean.

So how did ye get on down the office?

Ah've to call in at the end.

Albert lifted his nose up.

What's this?

Ah've asked the Credit Union for a sub.

We should've thought of that earlier.

Aye Ah know.

166

Albert looked at George.

D'ye think he'll get it?

No reason why he shouldnay. Been here long enough.

Did ye gie him a reference?

Aye.

He better pay it back then eh?

George laughed.

Got fuck-all to do with me, it'll come straight out his wages.

He had a look round the Junction and nodded.

If this place is clean boys, yeez might as well fuck off.

He grabbed the handrail of the steps and disappeared down and into Fresh. Albert called after him.

Have a good weekend boss.

And yerself.

They had a quick look to make sure the Junction was in order, then followed George into Fresh. They watched as he walked up to the girls in Fresh and called them for their payslips.

Uncle and nephew walked through Fresh and pushed through the door and into the corridor. They walked in silence. Sean scuffed his feet along the floor. They went into the cloakroom. Sean thought about the long bus ride home. The beer had worked down to his bladder.

Ah think Ah'll nip in for a piss.

Ah think Ah'll join ye.

They went into the toilet and stood next to adjacent urinals. Sean finished his before Albert. The old guy talked over his shoulder.

Ah swear as Ah get older my piss gets slower.

167

Sean pulled his cap off and stuffed it into his pocket. He looked in the mirror as he pulled his hairnet off and dumped it in the bin. He gave his hands a good wash and then his face and a wee bit of water onto his hair. He pulled his fingers through it and when he was happy looked at Albert.

How are ye gettin on there?

Albert looked over his shoulder.

This'll come to ye. Then ye'll be sorry.

Take yer time.

Go on ahead if yer in a hurry.

Sean looked at the door.

Aye right enough, Ah better get to the office.

Good luck then wee man.

Ah'll see ye at the bus stop.

Sean pushed through the toilet door and headed down the corridor towards the office. He hoped he didn't bump into Sammy. He couldn't handle any more threats. It didn't take long and he was in the heat of reception. The same lassie was typing away at her computer. He leaned on the counter and cleared his throat. She looked round and smiled. She wheeled her chair over to the counter and flicked through some files.

Here we are.

She pulled out a piece of paper with a envelope clipped to it. She separated the envelope and handed Sean the paper and a pen.

You need to sign for it.

Sean's heart pumped.

So Ah'm gettin it?

She nodded.

They'll take it back at a fiver a week. You'll not even notice it.

He signed and she handed him the envelope.

Hope it covers you.

Sean fondled the thick envelope.

Oh thanks doll.

Don't thank me. Ah just hand out the money.

Thanks anyway. This is got me out of some right trouble.

Glad we could help.

Sean turned to leave the office. He folded the envelope in half and tucked it into his back pocket. He couldn't help but smile. That was the money sorted. Everything should be alright now. He walked down the corridor and whistled.

He got to the main door and stepped outside. There was a gap in the clouds and the sun bounced off the snow and onto his face. He scanned the yard and held his hand over his eyes as he blinked. There was a sea of blue overalls milling around waiting for the buses that would take them home. Sean looked over to the bus stops and saw Albert at one. He was nearly at the head of a queue. Sean paddled through the crowd and joined Albert. Somebody called from behind.

There's a queue ye know.

Sean turned round. He cupped his hand over his eyes and scanned the horizon.

Where?

The person mumbled so Sean turned back to his uncle.

Alright Albert?

You're in a good mood.

Aye Ah know. They gave me the money.

That's magic son. Panic over eh?

A horn sounded and Sean and Albert looked at a car as it came alongside the bus stop. Sammy was driving and as he went past he looked at Sean and drew his finger across his neck. Sean gave him the fingers and the car stopped. The window went down and Sammy looked out.

What was that?

Sean nearly shat himself.

Eh nothin.

Ah didnay think so. See ye the night.

Sammy's tyres squeaked as he drove off. Albert turned to Sean.

Never mind son, ye'll have the pair of them out yer hair soon enough.

The bus came and people squeezed and jostled to get on. Sean heard his name being called. He turned round. It was Rab.

There's the wee boy.

Albert looked back and shouted.

Hurry up wee man.

Rab looked up and smiled. He put on a half-walk, half-jog. He looked tired and his work satchel kept falling off his shoulder and dragging along the ground. Albert looked at Sean and they both smiled and shook their heads. The queue pushed them towards the bus. When they got to the door, they stopped to wait for Rab. Sean shouted over the heads of the queue.

C'mon to fuck son, Ah want to get a seat on the bus.

People behind called for them to hurry up and get on. But they held firm. When Rab caught up, he handed Sean a plastic bag.

Here's the stuff ye left in my hut.

Sean took it and looked inside.

Cheers pal.

They got on the bus and continued straight up the stairs. They piled to the front seats but two white caps were in them. Sean signalled to them with his thumb.

That's our seat.

The white caps tutted but got up and moved to the seat behind. Sean slid into the window side. Rab sat next to him and Albert sat on the other side of the gangway. Sean reached into the plastic bag and pulled out the tobacco. He passed Albert his two pouches and a bottle of vodka. Albert nodded as he put them away.

Cheers pal.

Sean put his tobacco in his workbag, wrapped the plastic bag round the vodka and stuffed that in. He put the bag on the floor and leaned back into the seat with his arms crossed over his chest.

The bus swayed from side to side as it filled up. It was noisy in there. Always is on a Friday afternoon. When the driver started up, it was quiet for a minute. He gave it a few revs then they pulled away from the kerb. Everybody started talking again. Sean elbowed Rab in the side.

So who's the wee bird ye'll be seein the night?

Nobody ye'll know.

How d'ye know Ah'll no know her?

Coz ye'll no.

Sean never said anything for a bit. But he couldn't resist it.

No, who is she?

Rab looked ahead and nodded.

That's for me to know and you to wonder.

Fuck sake Rab ye sound like a wean at the school. Yer makin it up ya wee cunt.

No, am Ah fuck.

What's her name then? Pamela? Has she got a good grip? Ya fuckin wanker.

Fuck sake shut up.

Sean leaned into Rab and spoke quietly.

No, Ah'm only messin with ye son. Is she nice?

Rab looked around serious. His eyes were soft.

Lovely.

Sean patted his cousin's knee.

Best of luck to ye wee man.

He waited for a moment before calling his uncle.

Albert?

Albert lifted his head off the window.

What?

D'ye know that bird from Easterhouse? That fat one with the moustache and the glasses? Her that works in Packin?

What about her?

Your Rab's got her pregnant.

Rab elbowed Sean.

Shut up.

Sean held his side and tried not to laugh.

Fuck off ya cunt. Da, tell him.

Leave the boy alone Sean.

Alright.

Sean watched the edge of the road. The white line
flicked back and forward against the grass verge like a
bent railway line. He leaned his head against the window
and felt his teeth rattle in his head like a train going
over points. Archie's coming home, Archie's coming
home.

*

Ah'd been for this interview in Aberdeen. Ah was tryin
to get a wee job on the rigs. It was supposed to be
one of them two-day interviews with a night in a
hotel and back home the followin evenin. All expenses,
so it wasnay too bad. Thing was, as soon as the first
day was over Ah thought this isnay for me. Ah sat on
the bed in the hotel for half an hour, then Ah grabbed
my bags and headed for the train station. Ah couldnay
wait to get back to Royston. When the train pulled
into Edinburgh Ah had to change, so Ah thought Ah
might as well phone Maggie and she'd be able to get
some dinner ready for when Ah got in. Fuck knows
why but somethin stopped me. Ah thought Ah'd just
surprise her.

As soon as Ah walked off the platform at Queen
Street, Ah jumped in a taxi to get me to the house. As
Ah humped my bags up the path, Ah heard music from
the livin room. Ah thought it was a bit strange coz it
was about eleven o'clock. Ah pushed the key into the

173

lock and got my bags into the lobby. Ah was goin to shout on Maggie but Ah never. Ah just went straight into the livin room. Archie and Maggie were on the couch. He was pushin against her, tryin to kiss her, and he had his hand up her skirt. She was strugglin and Ah heard her tellin him no.

Ah turned the stereo off and shouted what the fuck's goin on. Archie turned round and said alright wee man. Ah couldnay believe the cheek of the cunt. He was tryin to ride my fuckin wife. Meanwhile she was pullin her skirt back down her legs. He just came round for a drink Sean she said to me. Ah telt them it looked like more than a drink to me.

Archie got up at this point and looked at his watch. Ah need to meet Sammy he said and went to leave. Ah was that angry with him Ah stood in front of him and asked what the fuck was he playin at. We've just had a coupla drinks he said. Ah'm sorry Sean it got a bit out of hand but ye know what it's like. Ah still stood there and looked at them. Ah wasnay sure what to do next. He said get out my way, Ah telt you I was sorry, so fuckin leave it. Ah stepped aside and he pushed past me and out the door.

Maggie sat there and looked at me. Ah checked out the empty beer cans and the upturned ashtray. Look at the state of this place Ah said. She started greetin. Ah'm sorry Sean. Ah saw him down the Co-op earlier and telt him ye were away for the night. She telt me he'd brought round a new steam iron and a bag of lagers. She'd let him in. He's my brother. She didnay think there was any harm in it. But when she'd had a bit to drink, he'd asked her for a cuddle. As a sister like, he'd said. She couldnay see any harm in it but as soon as he got his arms round her he started kissin her neck and tellin her he'd always fancied her. And it got worse. If Ah'd no come in, she didnay know what would have happened.

At that point she got up and grabbed me and cried her wee eyes out. It was the drink that done it. She begged me to forgive her.

Ah telt her there was nothin to forgive. Ah love Maggie. She's the centre of my universe. If anythin happened to her, Ah'd curl up and die. Thing is, Ah wanted to believe it was all Archie but my head started tellin me that he wouldnay have went round there if he didnay think he had a chance.

Ah didnay see him for a long while after that. The wean asked about him. Where was he? Ah got fed up hearin his name and one night Ah gave her a slap on the leg coz she wouldnay shut the fuck up about him. She just looked at me and ran up the stairs. Maggie gave me a look as well and ran up after her.

Ah thought Archie was avoidin me coz he never came round at all hours for a sandwich and a kip on the couch. It turned out he'd fucked off to England with Sammy and a coupla guys they knew from the Phoenix Tongs. One of Sammy's cousins telt me they were goin to make their fortunes out of hoors and crack. They didnay though.

Within six months one of the Tongs was dead and the rest of them were in the jail. Archie got a five stretch. It wasnay long before Ah got a letter from Lewes tellin

me how much of a good brother Ah was and would
Ah send him a tenner. And a pouch of tobacco. And a
coupla magazines. Ah was that taken aback with the
cheek of it, Ah sent them.

★

Sean's head was flicked forward when the bus halted.
He looked up and saw they were back in Glasgow. The
bus pulled away from the stop and he turned back to
the window and watched the red tenements slip past as
they got closer to Royston. The bus stopped and started
as it got caught in the city traffic. Albert and Rab gabbed
away about Friday night in the Fiveways.

Ah'm goin to do ye at pool the night.

Aye in yer dreams wee man.

Sean turned to Rab.

Ah thought ye were seein this lassie the night?

Ah am.

What, and yer takin her down the Fiveways?

Rab looked at his dad and then back to Sean.

What's the matter with that?

Sean looked at Albert.

And they say romance is dead?

Rab looked confused.

What would you know anyway?

Ah'd know better than to take a wee bird to the
Fiveways.

How, where would ye take her?

Ye could take her up the Scala. Get her onto the

176

back row. Throw some popcorn and ice cream into her. Before ye knew it, she'd be all over ye.

Albert nodded.

That's what Ah've been tryin to tell him.

Shut up Da.

Sean laughed again.

Don't tell yer da to shut up. He's giein ye good advice for fuck sake. Yer goin to be walkin home alone ye know. Ye might as well prepare yerself.

Rab's jaw stiffened.

Ah'm takin her to the Fiveways.

She'll no like it Rab.

But she wants to go.

Sean looked at Albert.

What sort of lassie wants to go to the Fiveways?

Albert looked out of the window. Sean pointed at him.

See son? Even yer da thinks she's a dog.

Rab looked at his dad and pointed his thumb at Sean.

Tell him Da.

Leave the boy alone Sean.

Sean rubbed his hands together.

So yer takin yer new honey to the Fiveways? This Ah've got to see. Ah'll definitely get a tenner the night.

Albert leaned forward.

Are ye sure Maggie'll let ye?

Rab laughed.

Aye Sean.

Sean turned to Rab.

Fuckin right she will. All Ah need to do is gie her the look. Her wee legs go to jelly and Ah can do anythin Ah want.

Rab laughed.

Listen to ye. Ah've no heard ye talk like that in front of her.

Sean winked at Rab.

Don't worry wee man. Ah'll be down there tonight inspectin yer new bird.

Rab scowled.

Ye better no fuck it up for me.

Fuck sake Rab. What d'ye take me for? Ah just want to see the wee lassie that's goin to take yer virginity.

Albert tried to be serious through his laughter.

Leave the boy alone Sean.

Rab looked really serious.

Ah'm no a virgin.

Aye ye are.

No.

Are.

Albert raised his voice.

Enough.

The bus trundled down the Royston Road and stopped opposite the park. Sean watched an old man's dog take a shite next to the entrance. He nudged Rab and pointed out the window.

Ye should tell yer girlfriend it's illegal to do that in public.

Rab tried not to laugh but he couldn't help it.

Ha fuckin ha.

The bus pulled away from the stop. An old drunk staggered up the pavement in front of them. He had wet patches on the crotch of his trousers. He looked as if he might fall in front of the bus. Rab nudged Sean and pointed at the tramp.

Ye should tell yer da to watch in case he gets ran down.

Sean looked at Rab.

That's no funny ya wee bastard.

Albert looked at Rab.

C'mon sir. There's a line now. Don't cross it.

Rab tutted and stared out of the front window. He leaned forward and Albert caught Sean's eye over Rab's back.

So where are ye meetin Archie?

Fuck knows. He'll probably turn up at the house at some point.

Rab leaned back.

What, is Archie about the night?

Sean nodded. Rab laughed.

Just what ye need. That mad bastard throwin a spanner in the works.

Sean looked at Rab.

Just watch the road.

Albert nodded at Rab.

He doesnay know any better.

Aye Ah know.

The traffic thinned out and the bus picked up speed. The Cadge Road stop appeared in the distance and quickly got closer. They gathered their stuff and made their way down the stairs. On the way down, Sean tapped Rab on the shoulder.

So where's she from, this what's her name?

She's from Sighthill.

Has she got tattoos?

Rab punched Sean on the sore thigh. Sean yelped and laughed.

Alright wee man, Ah'm only messin with ye.

They got off the bus and walked towards Cadge Road. Albert rolled a fag and put it in his mouth. He looked over his shoulder as him and Rab turned for the path.

So we'll see ye in the pub the night?

What time are yeez goin?

About eight.

Alright. Ah'll come down when Ah've sorted things out with Archie.

Chapter 13

Sean felt his guts heave as he looked up at the house and walked along the garden path. He could imagine her stood behind the curtains with her arms folded across her chest. He got to the front door and pulled his key from his pocket. He pushed into the lobby and smelled the fags as he walked into the house. He went through to the kitchen and she was sitting at the kitchen table. The kettle was just reaching the boil. He nodded.

Check that for timin.

He went through to the back lobby and hung up his jacket. He kicked his wellies off into the corner and put on his slippers. He went back into the kitchen and sat at the table. Maggie hadn't made any tea. She was sitting at the table.

Are ye goin to tell me what's goin on?

Ah suppose Ah better.

He got his pouch out and put it on the table.

D'ye want a fag?

She put her elbow on the table and rested her chin on her hand.

Never mind the fags.

Sean pulled tobacco out and made a slow fag. She tutted.

For fuck sake Sean.

Archie left me a load of money to watch when he was in the jail.

She sat upright.

And ye've spent it?

Aye but Ah've got it back.

That's alright then.

He picked at a stain on the table.

Ah'm sorry doll.

So how much did ye spend?

Seven hunner.

What on?

He rubbed his face with his hands.

Ah paid for Donna's school trip, did Ah no?

But ye said ye won that money in the bookie's.

Well Ah never. Ah took it out of Archie's stash.

But that trip was only two hunner.

He looked at her.

And Ah spent a bit on Christmas for yeez.

So it's our fault?

Ah never said that.

She looked at the ceiling.

Ye might as well have.

Well Ah never.

She folded her arms across her chest.

And ye never spent five hunner on our Christmas presents.

And the dinner and all the trimmins.

She looked at him with her head tilted to one side.

Still doesnay make five hunner Sean.

Well Ah spent a wee bit at the bookie's.

Ah might've known.

He tried to look really sorry.

Ah'm sorry doll.

She put one hand on her hip.

What am Ah goin to do with ye?

But Ah've got the money back.

Where is it?

He pulled the two hundred out and put it on the table. She picked it up and flicked through it.

There's no seven hunner here.

Sammy's got the rest of it, so there's no need to panic.

She tapped the wedge.

So where did ye get it from?

He told her.

Ye went to Albert? How am Ah goin to be able to look at him and Jessie?

She rested her head in her hand.

What about payin it back?

He told her.

Twenty-five pound a week? How are we goin to manage that?

Ah'll do some more overtime.

She stood up and went to the kettle.

Jesus Sean it's goin to be tight.

Tell me about it. Ah'm the one that'll be doin the extra work.

Ye should've thought of that before ye spent the money.

Sean put his fag in the ashtray as he stood up. He moved over to her.

Never mind a tea for me, Ah'm goin for a bath.

He tried to give her a cuddle but she pushed him away.

Yuck. Yer no touchin me with them scabby overalls on.

His arms dropped and he stood there like an awkward teenager. Maggie pointed to the washer.

Ye might as well get them off and Ah'll put them through the machine.

He stood by the sink and pulled his overalls and clothes off. Right down to his underpants. She tutted.

Put yer pants in as well.

He looked at her as he dropped his pants.

Any excuse to get me in the scud eh?

Aye alright handsome, just get them off.

She put his clothes in the machine.

Go and get bathed and changed

He climbed the stairs to the bathroom and turned on the taps. He sat on the side of the bath. The water came quick and steam soon filled the room. He put his arms in to swirl it around and the heat was strong. He climbed in. The heat tortured him as he eased deeper into the water. Then his bum touched the bottom of the bath and it was time for the best bit. Lean back and feel the hot water seep into his spine.

After a hard day ruling the masses, the Emperor relaxed and tried to ease out his aches and pains in a hot bath. His favourite concubine joined him. She appeared with a tray covered in chilled grapes. This didn't happen very often because back in them times they had no fridges and grapes tended to go off in the hot weather.

His concubine could make the finest cigars in the whole Empire. After he'd eaten the grapes, she brought out some tobacco leaves. She rolled a fat cigar on her thighs as she told him tales from the Kasbah and gossip from the harem. Then the Emperor leaned back and she lit his cigar. It was the greatest pleasure to relax in his extravagant bath with a hand-made cigar hanging from his lips.

He called downstairs.

Maggie?

What?

Could ye bring us up my tobacco and a can of beer?

She came up the stairs and into the bathroom. She handed him the beer and he popped it and took a swig.

Ah lovely.

She went to hand him his tobacco. He smiled.

Ye couldnay roll us one?

She made him a fag and lit it and passed it to him. He took a puff and rested back in the bath, fag in one hand beer in the other.

Cheers doll.

Is there anythin else or can Ah go now?

He winked at her.

Ah'm no finished with ye yet.

Yer all talk.

Do my back.

She dipped her hands in the water between his legs. He leaned forward and kissed her cheek.

Yer lovely ye are.

She grabbed the soap out of the tray and worked up a lather. Then she grabbed his shoulder.

Right come on.

He leaned over and she rubbed the lather into his back. He groaned.

Yer no a bad wee bath servant.

Ye think yer somethin special, so ye do.

Sean stretched his neck and groaned.

Ah do when Ah'm with you.

She tutted.

Smoothie.

He leaned back and smiled.

Do my chest.

She rinsed her hands in the sink.

Aye alright Sean.

She flicked cold water in his face and walked out of the bathroom.

Call yerself a wife? Get back here before Ah rise to ye.

He heard her laugh as she went down the stairs. He took a long draw on his fag and blew a smoke ring into the cloud of scented steam.

This is the life.

He sighed and took the last drag on his roll-up. He reached behind and flicked it into the toilet. It hissed as it hit the water. A last swallow and the beer was finished. He put the empty can by the side of the bath and searched for the soap. He found it and put it on the tray. Then he leaned back and relaxed. The world was not such a bad place. Everything was going to be alright.

But he couldn't relax for long. Thoughts of Archie irritated his brain as pinpricks of sweat burst through his forehead.

★

Me and Maggie were cuddled up in front of *Top of the Pops*. We'd just got Donna down and we were shattered. This was Maggie's favourite part of the day. When she could lie on the couch with me and we could have a bit of peace. Just the two of us. We were on the verge of a ride when somebody tried the front door. It was locked so they banged it. No just a light chap. A proper bang. Ah knew it was Archie. He opened the letterbox and called in. C'mon to fuck Sean. Pull yer breeks up and let me in.

He said he needed my help. Ah telt him Ah was busy but he said it was fuckin urgent. Maggie tutted but Ah knew Ah had to help my brother, so we left the house and got in the car. Maggie was at the window and she gave me some look. Archie wheel-spinned up the street and said Ah shouldnay worry about her. They're all the same. Treat them right and they come the cunt. They need to know who's boss. Tonight'll be a valuable lesson in the fact she's no the centre of the fuckin universe.

He asked if Ah knew what went on with Lizzie and a guy from Balornock while he was in the jail. Ah said Ah didnay know. Ah'd heard rumours but Ah was fucked if Ah was tellin Archie. Ah've saw him kill too many messengers to fall for that one. He looked me in the eye and asked if Ah was sure. Ah said Ah wasnay. He gave me a funny look but by this time we were pullin up in front of Lizzie's flat and he was distracted.

Lizzie looked rough as fuck. She had two black eyes and there was blood clotted round her nostrils. She looked at everything in the room but Archie. Ah could hear his breathin as Ah sat next to him on the couch. He made a roll-up and asked her for a light. Her hand shook that much he had to grab and hold it steady enough for his fag to catch the flame. He lifted his hand and she jumped, and he laughed and brushed his hair back. He looked at me and said that's the place to keep them.

Right, bell the cunt said Archie and she got on the phone. She telt the guy from Balornock to come round. She said of course it's alright, Archie was away in Edinburgh sortin somethin out. He was goin to be away for the night. Archie turned to me and snorted and straightened his neck. He flicked ash on the carpet and looked at her like she was goin to say somethin about it.

Archie pulled a broken bit of mirror from under the couch and asked me if Ah wanted a wee line of sulphate to get me in the mood for the evenin's entertainment. Ah thought Ah'd better, so we had one each, then he had another one. He asked Lizzie if she wanted one. She said aye, then he laughed and telt her she could fuck off. She looked at the carpet and said nothin.

Between rubbin his nose and swallowin snot, he telt me what was goin on. He'd heard about a guy sniffin round Lizzie while he was in the jail. After a bit of questionin, she had seen the error of her ways and telt him everythin. He'd gied her a bit of a slap for punishment and that, but had decided to forgive her. If it happened again but. She sniffed and said she promised it wouldnay. Fuckin better no he said.

Then he turned to me and telt me my job for the night. If the guy ran to the polis after his batterin, Ah was on hand as the only witness to the fact the cunt had attacked Archie and got hit back. The only defence was self-defence, know what Ah mean wee man? Ah nodded. Archie couldnay afford another conviction for serious assault. They'd gie him fuckin life this time. Simple.

Ah nodded to Lizzie. What about her? Archie looked at her and growled. She cannay be trusted at the minute. The best thing is for her to get away down her ma's. He gave her a tenner and telt her to get. She put her coat on and was on her way out the door when he called out. Make sure ye don't phone the cunt. She promised she'd go straight round her ma's.

Me and Archie sat on the couch and he asked how things were with Maggie. Ah telt him we were gettin on fine. Are ye sure? he asked. Coz ye cannay trust none of them. Wan thing the jail had taught him. When yer out of sight, birds fuck off to the next cunt throwin bread on the grass. They're fuckin hoors, the lot of them.

Ten minutes later the door went. Archie telt me to get it and he went into the kitchen. The guy was shocked when Ah opened the door but Ah telt him to come in. Lizzie was upstairs and he was to wait in the livin room.

He looked unsure but the thought of his hole got the better of him and he came in. Ah shut the door behind him and watched him sit on the couch.

What are ye doin here ye cunt? said Archie as he walked out of the kitchen. He had a baseball bat twitchin in his hand. The guy went to get up but Archie pushed him back onto the couch with the tip of the bat. The poor cunt looked at the door and Archie said yer goin nowhere ya cunt. He dragged a chair close to the couch and sat on it. He stared at the guy. Have ye got anythin to tell me? The guy shook his head. Sure? The guy nodded. Archie tapped his foot with the bat. C'mon son Ah'm sure ye've got somethin to tell me. The guy looked at me. Ah looked away. Ah felt a bit sorry for him but he'd made his bed so.

Archie banged him on the shin with the bat. Who came on to who? The guy said it was nobody's fault. They'd got drunk and it just seemed to happen. Archie cracked him on the knee with the bat and he went down on the carpet, rollin around holdin his leg. Just like that happened ya cunt shouted Archie, crackin legs and arms. He gave me the bat and nodded at the wounded lover. Ah gave the poor cunt a coupla half-hearted belts on the back. Archie kicked him in the guts and the head. Then he started laughin and pointin. The bitch has pissed herself he said and the guy started cryin. Listen to her, she's fuckin greetin like a wee lassie. Archie gave him another kick and started to unbutton his jeans.

Right cunt, if yer goin to act like a lassie Ah'm goin to treat ye like one. He telt me to pull the guy's jeans down. Ah grabbed the waistband and tugged them. The guy whimpered and tried to hold them up. Archie said for fuck sake and bent down and gave him a coupla punches. Then he grabbed the jeans and yanked them and yanked them till the bare arse was showin. The guy was shakin his head, cryin, goin no no no. He covered his ears with his elbows and bubbles of snot came out of his nose. Archie telt him to shut the fuck up ya dirty wee bitch.

Ah couldnay watch any more so Ah went into the kitchen. Ah heard him gruntin and callin the guy a tight wee cunt. It didnay take long and he started laughin, sayin the bitch is into it. Sean the bitch is into it. Ah came into the livin room and he was pointin at the guy's half a stauner. He called him a fuckin homo. Go on get yer fuckin kit on ye dirty fuckin hoor. He kicked him on the arse, and blood and spunk ran down his arse cheek and onto his thighs.

Archie said he was goin for a wash and Ah was to get that cunt to fuck before he stains the carpet. Ah said right son ye better get yerself the gether. The guy just laid there with his arms over his face. Ah reached down and grabbed his shoulder but he shrugged me off. After a bit, he stopped cryin and his hand reached down and pulled the back of his jeans up. He still had his face in the carpet and didnay get up till his arse was covered.

Ah helped him stand up. We were walkin towards the livin room door when Archie came back down the stairs. He had fresh clothes on. He looked and said ye make me sick ya fuckin dirty – and spat on him. Archie looked at me and said Ah thought Ah telt ye to get that cunt to fuck?

Ah helped the guy to the door and opened it for him. He limped down the path, still snivellin. When Ah went back into the livin room, Archie was sortin out another line of speed. We couldnay look at each other. Ah'm no a poof he kept sayin. It's just cunts like that do somethin to me.

Archie offered me a line of speed but Ah knew if Ah got too close to him Ah'd gag so Ah said no and sat on the chair. He had a coupla lines before he looked at me and when he did he wasnay my big brother any more. He looked right through me. He telt me what to say and what no to say. And there's certain things ye'll no tell any cunt, do ye know what Ah'm sayin Sean? Ah couldnay speak so Ah just nodded.

He gave me a tenner for my help and gave me a lift home. When Ah got out the motor, my hands were shakin like Lizzie's.

*

Sean reached for the shampoo and put a dollop in his hand. He rubbed it into his head and neck and ears. He tried not to get it on his face but it got there anyway. Right into his eyes so he had to keep them closed. He was starting to put the water on his head to rinse it off when he heard banging on the front door. He tried to reach for the towel to clear his eyes but it was nowhere to be found. He splashed water on his face and tried

192

to open his eyes but the soap stung so much he had to close them again. He heard the front door slam and shouting in the lobby. He heard someone banging up the stairs and into the bathroom.

So that's where yer hidin ya wee cunt.

He tried to get the soap out of his eyes and spluttered a reply. Cold hands grabbed the back of his neck and pushed his head towards the bath water. He resisted but the hands wriggled deep into his hair and gripped hard. He tried to grab them but his head went quicker into the water. He put his own hands down to the bottom of the bath and tried to push his head back into the air but the force was too great and his face stayed in the water. He started to struggle and felt the tension tear something in the small of his back. He couldn't breathe. He couldn't fucking breathe.

As quick as they grabbed his neck, the hands let him go and he managed to sit up. He sucked air into his chest and rubbed the lather from his face. Through his blinking eyes he could see a blurred image of Archie leaning on the wash basin.

Alright wee man?

Sean didn't know what to say. Maggie came into the bathroom.

What's goin on?

Archie lifted his hand and pointed to the door.

Get to fuck down the stairs. This is between me and him.

Sean wiped the last of the suds out of his face and turned to Maggie.

Get the money.

She turned and left the bathroom. Sean looked at Archie.

Alright brother?

Archie just stared at him. Sean put his hands on the side of the bath and braced himself to get out.

Stay where the fuck ye are.

Sean slumped back into the bath. Archie pulled a packet of fags out of his pocket and lit one. Sean looked at the dots tattooed on Archie's knuckles and the cigarette resting in nicotine-stained fingers. The hand moved to the face but Sean couldn't follow it. He looked down at the brand new trainers kicking against the skirting board. Archie picked up odd bits of bathroom stuff from the shelves and wash basin and put them back. He had a look in the cabinet then shut the door. Maggie came back with the money. She handed it to Archie. He took it and leaned back as he counted it. Sean looked at Maggie.

Go back downstairs love.

Maggie tightened her lips.

Suit yerself.

She left the bathroom.

Archie tapped the worktop with the cash and stared at Sean. Then he sprung across the bathroom and grabbed Sean by the hair on the back of his head. He shook him to the rhythm of the question he asked through his teeth.

Where's the fuckin rest?

Sammy's got it.

Archie nodded. He kept hold of Sean's hair with his left hand and took a few puffs on his fag. When its head was big and glowing, he held it in front of their faces and blew on it.

Oh aye?

Sean tried not to look at the fag-end but his eyes kept coming back to it.

He took it off me at work the day.

Archie took another couple of puffs on the fag. Sean felt the grip on his hair tighten. He found it hard to speak.

Yer no tryin it on with me are ye?

No, am Ah fuck. Ah swear on it.

Archie's eyebrows went up and he looked deep into Sean's eyes.

Ye fuckin sure?

Sean tried to nod but the grip on his hair was too tight. He squeaked out a reply then coughed. His head was pulled back till he could feel the pressure in his neck.

This isnay addin up wee man.

Sean smelled the fag before he felt the heat of it under his chin. He tried to wriggle away from it but Archie's grip was tight as fuck.

Ah swear on it.

Archie let his hair go with a flick. He stood up and looked out the window. Sean stretched his neck and rubbed it with his hand. He noticed a cigarette burn in the leg of Archie's tracksuit. Archie turned.

Ye better be tellin me the truth here.

He looked at the scar on Archie's face.

Ah swear on wee Donna's life.

Archie crouched down next to the bath.

Look me in the eye.

He flinched a wee bit but he did as he was asked. Archie grabbed him by the chin and stared right into him. Their auntie Jessie had said those eyes were beautiful. Sean thought they looked dead. He gulped and sweated, but he done it. He looked into the eyes and told him. Archie flicked his fag-end into the bath.

Right, Ah'm off. Don't get too relaxed wee man, coz if yer tellin me lies they'll be fuckin consequences. Have ye got that?

Sean nodded but couldn't look at Archie or say anything. Archie grabbed him by the hair again and twisted his face till they were close enough to kiss. His breath smelled of the jail.

Have ye got that?

Aye.

Archie let him go and stomped down the stairs. Sean heard the front door slam.

Maggie came into the bathroom. They looked at each other as a car started in the street and screeched away. Sean wiped the soap from his hair and face and reached for a towel. He looked at his wife.

Ah cannay handle this fuckin carry on.

Maggie grabbed the towel and passed it to him.

Well he's got his money now, so that should be it finished.

Sean stood up and started to dry his body.

Ah fuckin hope so.

Maggie lifted her arms up.

C'mere.

Sean climbed out the bath and they hugged.

Ah'm sorry.

She rubbed his back. She kissed his neck. He felt the heat enter his belly and his cock flicked against her jeans. She pushed him away and looked down. She looked at his face and smiled. The wee flush of red on her cheeks made her delicious. He smiled at her. She looked back at his cock.

Is that all ye think about?

He pulled her close and felt her hands tighten on his back.

Yer nothin but trouble O'Grady.

That's why ye like me.

He felt the lust course through his veins and he leaned in and smelled the hair next to her ears. He kissed her gently and her tongue snaked out. She bit his lip. She leaned back and he bit her throat.

That's lovely, she whispered.

His hands unbuttoned her and pulled the zip down. She grabbed his bum and ground her belly into his cock. He put his fingers in her waistband and felt her warm skin as he eased down her jeans. She wriggled her hips to help them down. When the jeans and knickers were halfway down her thighs, he turned her round and bit the back of her neck. She rubbed her bum in his groin and he bent his legs and felt the beautiful heat as he pushed his cock slowly into her fanny. She gasped and leaned forward onto the wash basin. He pushed harder and faster until she cried like she was hurt and he came twitching inside her.

They remained still for a while. Sean's breathing slowed and he coughed as a piece of catarrh tickled his throat. The cough bounced his cock out of her. He stood up. Maggie covered her fanny with her hand, and turned round.

Pass me a bit of toilet paper.

Sean passed it. Maggie wiped herself and pulled her jeans and knickers back up. Sean looked at his glistening cock.

Ah need another bath now.

They both laughed but Sean never had another bath. He just gave it a rub with the towel. Maggie watched with a grimace.

Dirty bastard, ye better bring that towel down to be washed. Get dressed and Ah'll make us some tea.

She left the bathroom and Sean smiled. He walked out of the bathroom and into the bedroom. He grabbed a pair of socks and a pair of boxers from his chest of drawers and sat on the bed, where he pulled them on. He sat there for a bit wondering what tracksuit to put on. He caught a glimpse of himself in the mirror and winked.

After a hard day making love with his numerous concubines, the Emperor often relaxed by sitting on the side of his bed with nothing on but his underwear. He cut a dashing figure that men envied and women found irresistible. He had perfected the sparkly-eyed smile that the camera loved. In fact if he hadn't been born to be the Emperor, he was sure he could have made a lot of money starring in pornographic films.

Maggie called from downstairs.

Tea's ready.

The Emperor pulled his tracksuit on and went downstairs. He swaggered into the kitchen and sat at the table.

He lifted the cup of tea nearest his seat. He blew on it and slurped some off the top. He had another slurp and put the cup on the table. Maggie pulled a fag from her packet and offered it to him. He put it in his mouth. She got one herself and lit it. She reached across with the lighter and Sean sucked the flame into his fag. He leaned back into his seat and exhaled the smoke towards the ceiling. He sighed loudly and had another suck on his fag.

Aye yer no a bad wee wife.

Maggie looked at him and her eyes glinted.

Is that right?

Sean felt a bit self-conscious, so he looked at his tea. He took a slurp and had more fag.

So when's the dinner?

Is that all ye think about? Yer knob and yer belly?

What else is there?

Yous men are like weans.

Aye when we're no puttin food on the table.

Maggie crushed her fag and smiled.

Ah could've done worse Ah suppose.

Fuckin right ye could've.

But then again Ah could've done a lot better.

Aye in yer dreams.

Maggie run her fingers through her hair.

Ah could've got myself a doctor or a dentist, and maybe got a wee bungalow out in Bearsden or somewhere.

A guy like that couldnay keep ye happy.

What are ye talking about?

If you had a guy like that, ye'd end up goin with the milkman or somethin.

What makes ye think Ah havenay already? For all you know, me and the milkman might be settin up a wee love nest up in the Campsie's.

What, with that ugly bastard?

Beauty's only skin deep ye know.

Aye and ugliness goes right to the bone.

Maggie laughed.

Yer that shallow, so ye are.

Sean tried to puff on his roll-up but it was out, so he sparked his lighter and lit it.

Ah'm shallow? Listen to ye goin on about guys with money. And anyway, if Ah was ugly ye wouldnay have looked at me.

Aye but Ah was only a young lassie then, Ah didnay know any better.

Yer fuckin unreal. Ye know how to make a man feel good about himself after ye've had yer way with him.

Maggie laughed.

Sorry, Ah forgot about yer wee male ego.

Have less of the wee.

Maggie looked at her watch.

Right, Ah better get the wean.

Does she no walk home with her pals?

Ah promised Ah'd get her a top for the youth club the night.

Sean pushed his chair back.

Ah'll walk down with ye.

Maggie looked shocked.

What, to the school?

What's up with that? She's my fuckin daughter isn't she?

They think Ah'm a single mother.

Sean laughed.

Fuck off. Ah was at the last parents' night.

That was over a year ago.

Sean scratched his head.

Was it? Fuck sake, time flies when yer a good father.

Maggie went into the back lobby.

Get yer jacket then if yer comin.

Sean followed her in. He picked his work jacket off a peg. Maggie snorted.

Yer no wearin that thing.

How no?

It stinks.

He hung it back up and grabbed his anorak.

Is that better?

She reached up and adjusted the collar.

Right, c'mon.

The two young lovers laughed and teased each other as they walked down the street. When they got to the end of Cadge Road, the sound of traffic filled their lungs. They turned into Royston Road and a lorry drove past. The exhaust must have been broken because it made the window in the newsagent rattle. Sean walked sideways along the pavement with his hand ahead to make a path through the people. He pulled his wife along behind him. They snaked between a woman pushing a pram and an advert stand for the local paper. The crowd thickened at the bus stop. He tried to find a space but the only way past was close to the kerb, where the draught from passing buses pulled at his hair.

Sean wanted to walk arm in arm with Maggie down the middle of the pavement. With nothing on but shorts and flip-flops and the flash of neon telling them they were in Spain. But he couldn't. It was winter in Royston and the streets were squeezing them into the gutter.

The crowd thinned as they passed the bus shelter. He could feel Maggie's grip on his hand as they approached the bookie's. The door opened and a man stumbled out. He dropped a cigarette end on the pavement and stood on it. He tucked his paper under his arm and looked down the road. His face lit up when he recognised Sean.

Alright wee man? How ye doin?

Sean felt Maggie tug harder on his hand.

No bad.

We've no saw ye for a while. Gave it up have ye?

Sean kept walking with the momentum of Maggie.

Aye. It's a mug's game.

The old man called after them.

Do what she says son.

They moved up the street before she said anything.

See? That's what happens. Ye don't want to end up like that do ye?

He focused on the end of the road.

No, do Ah fuck.

As they got closer to the school, a bell sounded. There was a Sunday-morning silence before the doors burst open and children streamed along paths like chickens through the Junction. The children were tired after a day being processed. A hard day that started when they were picked up by the ankles and given a good shake to make sure anything in their pockets fell out. Sometimes they were shook so hard, bits of their bodies fell off. They landed on the pile of catapults and loose change that gathered underneath them. When the pile got large and smelly, some guy appeared. He was an old guy too weak for the shaking. He swept all the droppings up. They were taken away by the council and ended up on a landfill site being picked over by crows.

The upside-down children are pulled through the school by a mechanical line. Some struggle and swear and spit on anyone who comes close. Some cry and hold bloody hands to their mouths. Some are already docile. Some even smile. There's no time to classify them though. Not in St Roch's. A computer pings them tumbling from the line onto a conveyor belt that travels through the basement. Tough arms grab them and pack them into individual steel cages. The stifled children are wheeled from the basement into an elevator. For a moment there is darkness until the door opens onto a long corridor with a black door at the end. Inside this room lives the Cheek Extractor. He wears a white suit and a dentist's smile. When a child arrives he holds up a syringe and says this may be uncomfortable. Before the day is out, the sparkle in the child's eyes has been mined and packed in a polystyrene box. It is now ready for shipment to a Californian plastic surgeon.

The smell of bubble gum and cheap perfume brought Sean back to the real world. He and Maggie moved to a pillar at the side of the gate where they wouldn't have

to struggle against the flow of children. The odd young-
ster would say something to Maggie. Sean thought they
looked familiar but he wasnay sure if it was them he
was recognising or their mums and dads. He felt Maggie
tighten beside him.

There she is.

Donna appeared with her pal. Sean pointed at their
interlocked arms.

What's goin on here then?

Donna's pal giggled. Sean winked at her.

Alright hen?

She nodded and looked at the floor. Donna frowned.

What ye doin here?

Can Ah no come and pick up my wee lassie from
the school?

Donna flicked her head at her dad and turned to her
mum.

Are we goin to the market then?

Maggie nodded. Donna put on begging voice.

Can my pal come?

Sean looked at the lassie.

Ah was hopin to get my daughter to myself the day.

Donna grabbed Maggie's arms.

Mammy?

Maggie looked at Sean and back to Donna.

Ye'll see her the night at the youth club.

Sean felt relieved.

Aye, and anyway, she'll feel a bit left out if you're
gettin a new top.

The lassie looked at Sean and back to the floor.

Can Donna stay round ours the night?

Donna spoke to her mum.

Aye can Ah?

Maggie looked at Sean.

What d'ye think?

Sean thought about it for a second.

Are ye goin straight home after the youth club?

Aye.

Well mind and no let me down.

They spoke at the same time.

We willnay.

And make sure ye stay the gether. There's some funny guys goin about at that time.

Donna tutted again.

What, ten o'clock? It's no that late.

Listen hen, d'ye want to stay out the night or what?

Donna looked sulky but she nodded.

Aye.

Well then do as yer telt.

The lassie spoke.

Ah'll make sure she's alright Donna's da.

Ah'm sure ye will hen.

He turned to Donna.

Right, c'mon you if ye want to get to the OK Corral.

Donna's pal looked at Sean.

What d'ye call it that for?

Coz when Ah was a boy ye never went to the market on yer own. Ye always had yer pals with ye just in case there was a fight.

Donna tutted and looked at Sean as if he was daft. She said cheerio to her pal and pushed in between her parents. The three of them walked up the hill towards the market. Sean felt a bit bad about telling the lassie to go home because there was lots of children heading for the stalls. Maggie turned to Donna.

So how did ye get on the day?

Ah got a row off my English teacher.

What for?

Their voices merged with the noise of the street. Sean kept one eye on his family and the other on the world. They passed a guy selling tobacco. He looked the sort that sold other stuff when he got to know his clients. Perhaps a bit of hash, or in special circumstances he'd nip up the flats to score a bag of brown.

The OK Corral had a reputation for sheltering fugitives from the law. And Sean saw one. A little guy lurking in a corner scanning for victims. Sean recognised him from school. He was a fast wee fucker. If he got hold of a pensioner's bag, there would be no chance of getting anything back. Within minutes the little bastard would be standing in an alleyway pocketing the cash and cards. If the old lady was lucky, the police would find a scattering of her sentimentals in a urine-stained corner.

The O'Grady family got closer to the market and Donna started to pull her mother's arm towards a brightly coloured stall. It was decorated with purple and pink tops attached to the roof with coat-hangers. A woman with orange foundation and gold jewellery stood at the edge. She was smoking a fag. She was hunched with the cold and not enough clothes on for the weather. She saw the O'Gradys approaching and dropped her fag. Her frosty scowl disappeared into a lovely smile.

What can Ah do for ye?

We're just havin a look.

Sean folded his arms as Maggie and Donna flicked through the clothes. He looked up and down the street. He met the eyes of the stall holder and gave her a nod and a white-lipped smile. The woman did the same back and started scraping hangers along a rail. Sean got his fag papers out and stuck one to his bottom lip. He pinched a fag's worth of tobacco from his pouch and rolled one up. He had just lit it when Donna touched Maggie on the arm and pointed to the roof of the stall. Maggie turned to the woman.

Gie's a look at one of them.

The woman reached up and ran her hands through the selection of vest tops hanging from the ceiling.

Ah'll see what Ah've got for ye.

Donna's eyes were glazing over.

Ah want somethin pink.

The woman selected a top and let Donna feel it. Sean felt himself edge away from the women. He kept finding his eyes straying towards the pub on the corner. The Fiveways was just up the road from here. He was choking for a pint.

It's thirsty work this clothes shoppin, so it is.

Maggie looked up from Donna.

Don't let us hold ye up.

Sean couldn't believe it.

What, d'ye no mind?

We'd get on better if ye werenay under our feet.

Sean looked at Donna.

At least ye'll be able to try a top on without my opinion. Eh hen?

Donna tutted and turned to the clothes. Maggie nodded to the post office.

We'll see ye there in half an hour.

She showed him her back as she rejoined the female huddle.

The homesteader had a long look at the womenfolk before heading for the saloon. Dodging through the townspeople on the pavement, he figured his wages should be in the bank. He approached the barred windows and popped his card in the autoteller. A quick look up and down the road and he pulled a ten-bill out the hole and tucked it into his wallet. He couldn't be too careful in these parts. Desperadoes were known to slice a man's belly for the price of a shot of whisky. He touched his belt as he walked round the corner. A hundred years ago men like him had guns to defend themselves against the roughs. Nowadays a strong right hand holding an empty bottle was the decider in many a neighbourly dispute.

He faced the double doors of the Fiveways saloon and hitched his tracksuit bottoms onto his hips. Then he took a deep breath and pushed on through. He almost turned and walked straight back out when he spotted the outlaw Archie O'Grady. The bad man and his partner were plotting no-good deeds from a corner seat. Sean thought about sneaking out but Archie saw him through the fag smoke and held up a half-empty pint of lager.

Talk of the devil and there he is.

Sean walked over to the table.

Alright boys?

He looked at Archie.

Did ye get the money?

What money?

Sean nodded to Sammy.

Five hunner pound.

Sammy and Archie looked at each other. Sammy turned to Sean.

What the fuck are ye talkin about?

Sean turned to Archie.

He's got yer money.

Sammy nudged Archie and they both laughed. Sammy pointed at Sean.

Got ye goin there son. Eh?

Aye nice one boys.

Archie lifted his pint.

D'ye want one?

Aye.

Archie pulled a tenner off a roll and dropped it on the table.

Get ours while yer up there.

Sean picked up the money and walked over to the bar. Sammy shouted after him.

And get me a packet of cheese and onion.

Sean looked at the barman.

Did ye hear that?

The barman nodded and got on with the pints. He grabbed the crisps out of a box on the floor and put them on the bar.

Four-ninety.

Sean gave him the tenner and picked up the drinks in a triangle. He took them over to the table and went back for the change and the crisps. When he got back to the corner, Archie and Sammy were drinking their pints but the other one was nowhere to be seen.

Right, come on to fuck, where's my bevvy?

Archie laughed and picked it up off a seat and put it on the table.

There ye go son. No sweat.

Yeez are a pair of comedians the day.

Sean had a sip on his pint and looked at the outlaws.

So what are yeez up to?

What are ye? The polis?

Just askin.

Sammy munched his crisps. Archie smoked a fag and leaned back in the corner. He looked at Sean but didn't say anything. Sean picked up his pint and had another swallow. He got his tobacco out and rolled a fag. He lit up and blew some smoke up to the ceiling.

So are ye glad to be out?

Sammy laughed and some bits of crisps hit the table.

What d'ye think ya stupid cunt?

They sat in silence for a long time. Sean started to wish he'd stuck it out at the market. It couldn't be worse than this. His head searched for something to say that wouldn't get laughed at or picked on.

Seen Lizzie have ye?

Aye Ah saw her earlier.

Alright is she?

Archie swept his fags to the side with the back of his hand and leaned across the table.

So what are ye up to the night?

Ah was goin to come down here with Maggie.

Cannay see that happenin.

What are ye talkin about?

Ah might have a wee drivin job for ye later.

Sean flicked his fag ash onto the floor.

But Ah'm takin Maggie out.

Archie leaned further over the table. His forehead seemed to come down over his eyes.

Ye owe me wee man.

Ah paid all yer money back.

Archie held up his finger.

Aye but ye spent it.

Ah got it all back.

That doesnay matter. While Ah was in the jail, you were enjoyin yerself at my expense.

But Ah was doin ye a favour.

Archie looked at the window for a second. He exhaled a deep breath and turned back to Sean.

When ye were short of money, Ah gave ye a job did Ah no?

Sean nodded.

And when ye got into trouble with them bookies, who got ye out of it?

You.

And when ye were supposed to be watchin my cash, what were ye doin with it?

Sean never said anything.

So what are ye doin the night?

Sean nodded at Sammy.

How come he cannay do it?

Archie wrapped his hand round his pint glass.

Me and Sammy have got a bit of business to attend to.

Sammy laughed. Archie took a drink.

We've got some debts to pull in. Ye could take Sammy's place if ye think ye've got the balls.

Sammy sniggered. Sean gulped so that he could speak like a man. He looked at a fag smouldering in the ashtray. Archie picked it out and crushed the last of the smoke out of it.

What's it to be then wee man?

Sean tutted like Donna.

Alright.

Archie pushed the change from the last round over to Sean.

Good. Now that's sorted, get another drink in.

Sean grabbed the money and stood up.

And Sean?

What?

Better get yerself a Coke. Don't want ye gettin done for drunken drivin.

Sammy laughed.

Drunken drivin. That's a good one.

Sean got the drinks and came back to the table. He passed a drink to Sammy, who got his fags out and gave the brothers one each.

Yer a good driver Sean. Pity we didnay have ye in the cockpit that night we went to Falkirk.

Archie pointed at Sammy.

Ow. Watch it.

No, but he is.

Archie slapped Sean on the shoulder.

Aye he is. But he's my wee brother, so he's bound to be good at something.

Sean smiled despite himself. He had a last swallow on the lager before he moved to the Coke.

So where's the delivery?

Ah'll tell ye later.

Ah'll just do the one, alright?

Archie and Sammy looked at each other. Archie took a blast on his fag.

It isnay that simple wee man.

Can ye no get anybody else to do them?

Sammy laughed.

Oh aye. We could get loads of guys. But half the cunts would run to the police and the other half would disappear with the goods.

Archie slapped Sean on the arm.

It'll no be long. We'll have somebody else in a couple of months.

So how come he cannay do them now?

The wee bastard's in Glenochil. He'll no be out till April.

What am Ah goin to tell Maggie?

She's yer wife isn't she? Just get her telt.

Sean sighed and had a swig on his Coke. It wasn't very tasty. He pushed it away and went to stand up.

So when d'ye want me?

We'll gie ye a bell later.

Sean nodded to the barman on his way past.

When he stepped outside, he noticed it was getting dark. He pulled his jacket close and headed down the street. He saw a movement at the side of the pavement and realised it was an old man hunched up on a set of steps. He had a blanket round his shoulders and a can of beer by his side. The guy asked him for the time. Sean stopped.

It's about half four.

Have ye got ten bob for a cup of tea son?

The old man's eyes lit up as Sean searched in his pockets. But all he had was four pence. He handed them over.

Sorry pal that's all Ah've got.

The old man turned the coppers over in his palm and muttered something. Sean felt bad. He didn't know whether to give the guy the tenner from the machine or tell him to get a fuckin job like the rest of us. Sean turned and walked down the road. He heard the coppers jingle on the pavement. The old man called after him.

Stick yer money ya tight-arsed cunt.

Sean kept walking.

He got to the post office and the lassies were waiting for him. He pointed at Donna's plastic bags.

So what did ye get?

Donna swung the bags.

A top and some make-up.

Magic.

Maggie grabbed Sean by the arm and whispered in his ear.

Where are ye takin me the night then?

Sean felt cold air hit his eyes as he fixed them on the street ahead.

We need to talk about that.

She let his arm go.

How come?

Sean coughed to clear his throat.

Ah'm doin a wee job for Archie.

Maggie looked disgusted.

Jesus Sean.

She walked ahead and linked her arm into Donna's. Sean put his hands in his pockets as he followed. He kicked a stone across the pavement. It hit the kerb and twitched and bounced into the road.

CHAPTER 14

He opened the front door and stood in the hall. Donna rushed straight into the living room and turned the telly on. After Maggie came in, Sean closed the front door. He went into the back lobby and hung up his jacket. When he got back through, Maggie was leaning on the door jamb looking into the living room.

Get yer mucky feet off the furniture. Tell her Sean.

Listen to yer mammy.

Donna took off her shoes and put them at the side of the couch.

And don't tut at me said Maggie.

Donna leaned towards the telly and turned it up. Maggie looked at Sean, pushed her body from the door and walked into the kitchen.

Suppose Ah better start cookin. Nobody else is goin to do it.

Sean gave the door the fingers. He turned to the living room and noticed Donna watching him with a smile on her face.

What's wrong with her?

Christ knows.

Donna turned to the telly. Sean picked at his knuckle.

Did she say anythin on the way home?

She didn't turn away from the telly.

No.

He didn't look up from his knuckle.

Don't be gettin too attached to the telly missus. Ye'll need to get changed out of that uniform so it can get washed for Monday.

He went into the kitchen and sat by the table while Maggie prepared the dinner. He watched the muscles on the back of her arms twitch as the knife scraped the peel off the potatoes.

Ah'm sorry doll.

Maggie faced him.

Ye should tell him to get somebody else.

Ah tried but −

It's about time you put me and Donna first.

She turned her back on him and got on with peeling the potatoes. He looked at her and knew they had to get out of here. Move to England, or somewhere a bloke could have half a chance at a decent life. Maybe get a wee house like the ones next to the factory. In some of them places down south they have council houses in the middle of nowhere. They've got huge gardens with roses climbing up the walls. Nice wee hedges. Maybe a greenhouse full of tomatoes. A washing line with white sheets hanging from it. And good schools where the kids have a desk each and the teachers can give them a bit of time.

Ah'll phone Gambo.

Maggie dropped a potato into the sink.

D'ye think he'll be able to sort it out?

Ah fuckin hope so.

He sat at the table and made himself a roll-up. He took his time with it. Made sure it was perfect. He lit it and had a couple of slow puffs. Maggie turned from the sink.

Ah thought ye were goin to use the phone.

He looked at her through the smoke.

Right.

He felt like an old man as he got up from the table and went through to the living room.

Ah need to make a phone call hen.

Don't let me stop ye.

In private.

But Ah'm watchin this.

Sean growled.

Just get out the fuckin way.

She slammed the door on her way out. He heard her stomp up the stairs and her bedroom door bang shut.

He had a deep drag and picked up the phone. He dialled half the numbers, let a puff of smoke out, then dialled the rest. It rang a couple of times before a woman answered.

Baird Street.

Would there be any chance of speakin to Detective Sergeant Gambol?

I'll see if he's in the building. Who shall I say is calling?

Sean wanted to put the phone down at that question, but he never.

Sean O'Grady.

The phone went quiet for a bit. Then it clicked and rung twice before it was picked up.

Gambol speaking.

Alright Gambo? It's Sean.

Alright wee man?

No, no really.

What's up?

Can we talk?

Aye talk away son.

Archie's back.

Have ye spoke to him?

Sean's toes dug into the carpet.

Aye.

What about?

The money he left me when he went in the jail.

Sean heard Gambo laughing.

Have ye spent it ya prick?

Aye but Ah got it back.

Gambo laughed some more then stopped.

Does he know about our wee secret?

No, Ah shouldnay think so.

What's the problem then?

He's asked me to do some deliveries.

There was a couple of seconds' silence before Gambo
spoke.

So?

Sean blew smoke into the handset.

Ah don't want anythin to do with them.

Well tell him to fuck off.

Easier said than done.

Gambo laughed again.

It is with that cunt.

So what am Ah goin to do?

When's the first delivery?

Sean looked out the window.

The night.

Where?

Ah don't know exactly. They'll phone me later with the details.

Hold the line a minute.

Sean didn't just hold it. He played it round his fingers into little knots.

Sean?

Aye.

Ah'll set up a wee team. Gie's a bell when ye know what's happenin.

OK.

The phone went dead and Sean put it down. He sat next to it, smoking and gazing at the wallpaper.

★

Ah was strugglin with money. Maggie didnay have a job at the time and the factory work didnay seem to cover all the expenses. It was a choice between new shoes for the wean or a coupla beers after work on a Friday. Fuckin nightmare coz ye have to buy the shoes but at the same time yer hangin out for a pint. Especially when all yer mates are havin one. Ye end up takin out wee loans with the provvy just so ye can have a drink. Before ye know it, yer neck-deep in shite.

Ah went to see Archie coz he seemed to be doin alright. He was drivin a Golf GTi and he always seemed to have loads of dosh. Ye havenay got a wee job Ah could do for ye? Ah asked him. He gave me a look and laughed and said no. Ah begged him. Telt him Ah'd do anything. He looked at Sammy. Gie the boy a wee earner said Sammy. Archie said he'd think about it.

A coupla weeks later Ah got a phone call off Sammy. He said Ah was to meet him outside the garages at the end of the street. He pulled up in a motor and telt me to get in. We drove back near his. On the way he telt me there was a packet under the seat Ah was to take to a house in Penilee. The guy in the house would gie me a parcel to bring back. It shouldnay take me more than an hour. If everythin went alright, he'd gie me fifty bar when Ah got back.

The journey went OK and that weekend Ah took Maggie out for a wee drink. Easy money Ah thought, so Ah started droppin packages off once a week. Ah'd meet up with guys in car parks or service stations and swap parcels with a nod of the head and say hello to yer brother. Sometimes Ah got close to Edinburgh. Maggie started to notice that Ah had more money. But Ah just telt her Ah was doin a wee bit of overtime and took her out now and again. That kept her quiet. Ah was even takin drivin lessons.

One Friday a polis stopped me. He asked me my name and Ah gied him a false one. He radioed it in and everythin seemed sweet until this CID motor drew up. Ah almost didnay recognise him coz he'd put on so much weight. All Ah saw was a fat boy gettin out and sayin Sean, what have ye been up to? The traffic copper said Sean, Ah thought yer name was

John? Fuck sake Ah thought, and looked at the CID. It was Gambo. Ah asked him if Ah could have a word in the motor.

He asked me what the fuck was goin on and who the fuck was John Brady. Ah telt him Ah was drivin the motor without a licence and could he gie me a break. At first he wasnay havin it. Said he'd have to report me. But Ah begged him. Gied him the old-pals act. He wasnay even standin for that so Ah mentioned the fire Ah dragged him out of when we were weans. He went a bit quiet. Looked at his nails and pressed round them with his car keys. Alright Sean he said.

He telt the traffic cop Ah was an important snout of his and Ah was on a job that shouldnay be interrupted. As quick as ye can say Mason's handshake, the deal was done and dusted and Ah was free to deliver my package. Well no quite. Gambo wanted a wee word before Ah went.

He got back into the motor and asked me what the fuck Ah was up to. Ah said thanks for doin me the favour but Ah couldnay say anything. He asked if Ah was doin some runnin for Archie. Ah shook my head but he didnay believe me. He said Archie was gettin too big for his boots and Ah should stay clear, coz before long they were goin to nick him.

Gambo got out the motor and was about to close the door when he pulled it back open and poked his head in. He pointed at me. Ye've been lucky this time Sean. Lucky Ah was passin and lucky Ah didnay forget a good deed. It's paid now though. Ye'll be on the same terms as any other cunt the next time we meet, so if ye ever need a favour from me remember they'll be a price to pay. Ah nodded but didnay say anything.

★

Sean got up from the telephone and went back through to the kitchen. He sat by the table while Maggie prepared the dinner.

Well that's my bed made.

Ah heard.

She lifted the lid off the boiling potatoes, looked inside, and put the lid back on. Sean shuddered at the sound of the metal lids scraping the sides of the pans.

Sean reached for his roll-ups. He hunched over the pouch as he rolled a fag.

Archie's goin to kill me when he finds out about this. Maggie sat opposite Sean and reached out to touch his hands.

By that time he'll be in the jail.

Ah'm feart he'll get it out of me before.

How?

Sometimes Ah get the feelin he can look into my eyes and tell exactly what's goin on in my head.

Maggie dropped Sean's hands.

Don't be daft.

No seriously. Ever since we've been kids Ah've felt it.

Next thing ye'll be tellin me he can see into the future.

Sean laughed.

Christ knows why Ah'm laughin, coz Ah'm shittin myself.

Maggie reached her hands out again.

It'll be alright. This time the morra we'll be sittin here safe and he'll be locked up where he belongs.

Ah fuckin hope so.

The potatoes hissed. Sean looked and saw a head of foam travelling down the side of the pan and onto the cooker. Maggie got up and turned the gas down. She lifted the lid off the mince and stirred the pan with a wooden spoon. She tested the potatoes with a fork.

These are nearly done.

She went into the pantry and brought out a tin.

Beans she said.

Aye lovely said Sean.

Maggie opened the tin, pulled another pan from under the sink and poured the beans into it. She put the pan on the cooker and clicked on the gas.

Five minutes. Gie Donna a shout.

Sean got up and went into the lobby.

Donna.

Aye Daddy.

Yer tea's about ready.

Ah'm comin.

Sean went back into the kitchen and got three plates out of the cupboard. He put them on the worktop next to the cooker. He went into the cutlery drawer and got three sets of knives and forks out. He put them in the middle of the table. He got a bottle of brown sauce, the salt and a bottle of tomato ketchup out and put them next to the cutlery.

Ye've forgot the spoons said Maggie.

Sean looked at the cutlery on the table.

Oh shit. Sorry love, Ah'm good for fuck-all the day. He pulled three spoons out of the cutlery drawer and put them next to the knives and forks on the table. He got three bowls out of the cupboard and put them on the draining board. He went into the pantry for a tin of Carnation milk and a tin of peaches. He opened the peaches and shared them between the bowls. Then he opened the milk and poured it over the peaches.

Peaches and cream he said.

Aye lovely.

Maggie put piles of steaming food on the plates. Sean went into the lobby and called up the stairs.

Donna.

What?

Yer fuckin tea's out.

Aye OK, Ah'm comin.

Well get a move on.

Sean went back into the kitchen. The plates were on the table and he realised he was starving. He pulled his chair out and sat next to the biggest pile of food. He poured a load of salt on it and splattered a dollop of brown sauce on the side of his plate. He dug his fork into the mince and it was on its way to his mouth.

Careful it's hot said Maggie.

Sean blew on his mince for a bit and put it in his mouth. It was hot. He breathed air into his mouth to cool it down. He swallowed it. He should let it cool for a bit but he was so hungry he had to have some more. Donna joined them at the table. She grabbed a fork and dug it into the mince.

Careful it's hot said Maggie.

Donna looked at her daddy.

It's fuckin roastin said Sean.

Donna picked a little mince on the end of her fork and blew on it. She put it in her mouth and coughed.

It's roastin she said.

Ah telt ye said Sean.

Ye'd be complainin if it was cold said Maggie.

Sean laughed and nodded at Donna.

Aye.

Shut up Dad.

So are ye lookin forward to the night?

Donna's eyes almost glazed over.

Aye.

Ah hope ye don't disappear up the toon dancin.

Shut up Dad.

Sean looked at Maggie.

D'ye hear that?

Aye Ah know. God knows where she gets it.

Maggie looked at Donna and they burst out laughing. Sean thought they were laughing at him. He tried a forkful of food and it was cool enough so he started shovelling it into his mouth. Before long he was scraping the last of his dinner from his plate. He watched Maggie and Donna finish theirs, then collected their plates and put them in the sink. He put the pudding in front of them.

Would madam like some more cream?

Shut up Dad.

The pudding was ate and Sean put the dishes in the sink. He re-boiled the kettle and made them a cup of tea each. He went into the pantry and took out a packet of chocolate biscuits. When they had finished, he stretched and nodded Donna to the sink.

What? she said.

Dishes.

Oh Dad.

Listen, if ye want any money for the youth club, best ye get them dishes done.

Donna tutted but she got up and got on with the dishes. Sean reached over and touched Donna's arm.

And watch that knife hen. It's fuckin sharp.

Donna pulled the knife out of the sink. She washed it with exaggerated care. Sean looked at Maggie.

She'll no be laughin when she's missin a finger or two.

Maggie opened her fag packet and offered it to Sean.

Don't mind if I do young lady.

Donna tutted. Maggie got her lighter and gave them both a light. They sucked their fags and pushed their backs into the chairs. Sean patted his belly.

Aye ye always feel better after a bit of dinner.

Maggie smiled at him. The phone went and Sean's heart pumped and he felt his dinner burn into his guts. Donna wiped her hands.

Ah'll get it.

Sean stood up.

No, leave it.

Donna ignored him and went into the lobby.

But it'll be for me she said.

Donna, what the fuck did Ah tell ye?

Sean pushed past her and went into the living room. He pulled the door closed behind him. He sat at the telephone table and took a breath. Then he picked the phone up, put it to the side of his head, and spoke.

Hello.

Is Donna there?

What?

Eh is Donna there?

Hang on.

Sean went back into the kitchen.

Donna, it's for you.

Donna gave him a look down her nose and waltzed out of the kitchen. Sean felt shite. The heartburn was travelling up his throat and threatening to explode out of his mouth. He sat down and leaned his elbows on the table.

Ah cannay take much more of this.

Maggie stopped drying the dishes and came over and put her hands on his back. She rubbed his neck and shoulders.

Maybe ye should have a wee can of lager.

My guts are killin me. A can might make me boak.

Well have some milk.

Maggie went into the fridge and brought out a half-empty bottle of milk. She handed it to Sean.

Go on.

Sean took the bottle and had a wee sip. His guts churned and he rubbed them with his hand. Maggie picked up a pan and wiped it with the dish towel.

Go and watch some telly. That'll take yer mind off it.

Sean got up and went into the living room. When he got there, Donna was sitting on the couch watching *The Simpsons*. Sean sat beside her.

Who was that on the phone?

Just one of my pals.

Oh aye?

Aye.

Sean winced as he sipped the milk.

Are ye off to the youth club then?

Aye.

When?

In a minute.

Ye'll be wantin some money then eh?

Donna turned round with her hand out.

A fiver.

A fuckin fiver. Do ye know how much pocket money Ah used to get?

Donna rolled her eyes.

Ten pence she said.

Sean laughed at her cheek.

It's no funny.

Have ye never heard of inflation?

Sean pulled his wallet out of his back pocket and drew out the tenner. She snatched it out of his hand and done a wee dance around the living room carpet.

Thanks Daddy.

Go and ask yer ma for change.

Sean picked up the remote and started flicking through the channels. Just the usual shite to watch. He would get bored with a programme within a minute and flick to the next one. Donna came back into the living room and done more dancing. This time she had a fiver in each hand. She gave one to Sean

Dad?

What?

Do ye need the toilet?

When did ye become interested in my bowel movements?

Yuck, that's disgustin.

Why are ye askin then?

Coz Ah'm goin for a bath.

Oh right. Go ahead but try no to use all the hot water. Remember yer ma'll want one as well.

Sean got back to the telly. He had a slurp of milk and felt it ease the burn in his guts. He leaned back in the couch and made a fag. A wildlife programme came on. The Serengeti. A cheetah family on the verge of starvation. Daddy cheetah's been shot by poachers and his feet are for sale in some market in Lagos. Mammy cheetah was a single parent on the savannah with two youngsters to bring up. And one of them was sickly. Poor wee thing was limping a bit and didn't get full shares of the grub.

Laws of the jungle Ah suppose said Sean to the telly. Mammy cheetah hid her kittens in a cave halfway up a cliff. She went hunting for a bit of gazelle for the Sunday dinner. The camera panned onto a young gazelle tottering beside its mother. Mammy cheetah sneaked up as far as she could. Her shoulder blades swivelled as she pushed through the high grass. Every now and then the gazelles stopped and put their noses in the air for a sniff. The cheetah stopped too. Then she broke through the grass and ran at the awkward wee gazelle. It didn't see the cheetah. It was too busy playing with a butterfly. It sensed something and looked for its family. But they've already run. For a moment the camera zoomed in on its eyes. Pure terror. The wee gazelle tried to run and dodge but the cheetah had being doing this for years. It swiped the back legs and the gazelle tumbled to the floor. The cheetah grabbed it, tumbled with it and bit into the back of its neck.

The phone went and Sean twitched and spilled milk down his hand. He put the bottle on the coffee table and wiped his hand on the back of his tracksuit as he walked to the phone. A quick draw on his fag and he picked the phone up.

Sean?

Sean's pulse beat in his throat.

Aye.

Be at the Fiveways in ten minutes.

Sean opened his mouth to answer but the phone went dead. He couldn't even say who it was. Archie or Sammy or somebody else.

He put the phone down and rested his hand on it for a few seconds. Then he picked it back up and dialled Gambo's number.

That's fuckin excellent Sean. We'll have the cunt under lock and key before the night's out.

Ah cannay say Ah feel good about this.

Get real wee man, coz at the end of the day it's either you or him.

What are ye tryin to say?

We're always goin to go for cunts like Archie. It would

231

only be a matter of time before we caught up with yeez. And who d'ye think we'd get first?

Sean never said anything.

The delivery driver. One night we'd grab ye with the gear in the motor and it'll be cheerio Sean. Who'll look after the family then? Archie? Ah think not.

Aye maybe.

There's no maybe about it. If Ah don't hear from ye later, Ah'll assume ye've swapped sides and ye'll be as much of a target as him.

There's no need for threats.

There's every need. This is a war wee man, and Ah don't take prisoners, so yer either on my side or ye arenay. What's it to be?

Ah'll phone ye later.

Make sure ye do.

Sean put the phone down. He sighed. Then he put his hands on his knees and pushed himself to his feet. He stood there and stretched.

Maggie came into the living room.

Was that them?

Aye.

She gave him a cuddle.

See ye later then.

He tried to make a joke.

No unless Ah get killed.

She wasn't laughing.

That wasnay funny. Ah'll see ye here the night.

He gave her a last kiss.

See ye.

He went through to the lobby and shouted up the stairs.

Donna.

Λye.

Ah'm away out.

What are ye tellin me for?

Just. Nothin. Have a good time at the club.

He turned the latch, pulled the front door open, and walked into the night.

CHAPTER 15

The car park was dark. There was a Ford Escort half hidden under the drooping branches of a hawthorn tree. Sean headed for it. He could tell there was someone inside the car by the glow of two cigarettes. As he got closer he realised the window was rolled down and there was an elbow poking out. Closer still and he could make out Archie's face in the driving seat. Sean crossed to the motor and hunched down next to Archie's window.

Sammy looked at his watch and leaned across from the passenger seat.

Yer timin's shite wee man.

How? Ah'm here in less than ten minutes.

Are ye fuck, yer two minutes late.

Sammy opened the door and swung himself off the passenger seat. He stood next to the motor with one hand on the door and the other on the roof.

Right Archie, Ah'll see ye a bit later.

Archie slid across from the driver's seat to the passenger's seat.

Alright pal. Remember what Ah telt ye.

Aye no problem big man.

Sammy closed the door and looked through the motor to Sean.

See ye later wee man.

Archie turned to Sean.

Get in.

Sean got in the car. He adjusted the seat and checked the key was in the ignition.

Where to?

Head down the Royston Road towards Germie.

Sean drove out of the car park and kicked the motor up through the gears.

Nippy wee motor.

Aye.

Sean dropped into third for a corner and the wheels screeched on the way round. Archie growled.

Take it easy ya stupid cunt.

Sean let off the accelerator and checked the mirrors.

So where are we off to?

Ye'll find out when we get there.

They drove down the road and a car pulled out of a junction and came up behind them. Archie reached for the sun visor and pulled it down. He looked in the vanity mirror.

Ah hate cunts like that, drivin up yer arse.

Sean looked in the mirror.

Aye Ah know.

They came to Germiston and Sean looked at Archie.

Just keep to a steady thirty. Straight ahead.

Sean reached over and turned the radio on.

A wee bit of music eh?

Archie reached over and turned it off. They drove in silence for ten minutes.

Next left.

The motor behind them carried on the way it was going. Archie turned in his seat and had a look behind them. They drove into a scheme Sean hadn't been in since he was a kid. Archie directed him with so many lefts and rights Sean ended up not sure where they were. They came to a bit where pensioners or people who cared about the street lived. Well-kept gardens with trimmed hedges and roses. Half-decent motors on the road and no youngsters leaning on lampposts or playing football.

Stop next to that Neighbourhood Watch sign.

Sean stopped. Archie got out of the car.

Get out.

Sean got out and locked up. Archie nodded towards the motor.

Put the key behind the front wheel and follow me.

They walked down a cycle path until they came to a road with elm trees and long driveways. There was a Fiesta XR2 next to the exit of the cycle path. Archie pointed to the front wheel.

Keys are there.

Sean bent down and got the keys, opened the door, and started it up. He looked at Archie.

Where to now?

Head for the Blackie.

Sean laughed.

Bandit country.

Just fuckin drive.

He drove to Blackhill and on the edge of the scheme found a phone box. Archie got out and made a call. Sean waited. He wondered why Archie didn't use his mobile. After a minute at the most, Archie ran out of the box, hands holding his pockets, and climbed back into the motor.

Drive down to the end and pull a left.

They turned into a road full of old cars. A gang of lads in tracksuits hung around the entrance of a single tower block at the end of the street.

Pull over behind that transit.

Sean stopped and Archie got out the car.

Ah'll be ten minutes.

He slammed the door and swaggered up the path. He nodded to the lads and disappeared into the flats.

Sean turned on the radio and skinned himself a fag. He rolled the window down an inch or so, sparked the fag up and flicked the still-smoking match into the street. The fag was puffed till it was a soggy half inch between Sean's fingers. He reached for the open window and dropped it outside. An Alsatian-type dog appeared at the side of the flats. In the distance it could have been a wolf. It loped through the communal gardens in a zigzag with its nose in the air. Something caught its attention and it darted to a fence, where it had a root about. It tore something from the ground and chewed. It twisted its head as it tried to swallow. Somebody walked out of the flats and the door banged behind them. The dog twitched sideways at the noise before resuming its search. It sniffed the corner of the tower and had a piss before it disappeared into the snowy waste.

The scheme was like something from an old black and white spy film. Concrete flats sprouting out of the tundra to house the workers of the Siberian oilfields. Nothing to do but work and drink and try to keep warm. Sean waited in the car as the Russian mafia counted their cash in a flat occupied by a single mother. Sometimes the gangsters would lace her with drink. They would take turns at fucking her while her children pretended to sleep in the next room. They would give her fifty roubles at the end of the deal and she'd be able to buy food and coal to keep her going till her next welfare cheque.

Sean rolled another fag as a woman with a fur coat and high heels walked up the street next to a boy on a mountain bike. She had a nice pair of legs. They walked past the motor and Sean watched them in the mirror till he heard a noise. He looked to the flats and saw his brother coming down the path. He turned the radio off as Archie climbed into the car with a Tesco carrier bag in his hand. He held it open so Sean could see the contents.

There's four grand in there.

Archie took another wad of notes out of his pocket and put them in the bag.

That's five all the gether.

Sean thought about the start him and Maggie could have in England with five grand. He looked in the bag again.

That's a lot of money.

Yer fuckin right it is.

So where did that come from?

238

Archie touched the side of his nose.

Polis are ye?

D'ye have to gie them it back?

Fuckin right Ah will. And another two on top. Just as well junkies are such good thieves or Ah wouldnay be able to afford it.

Sean laughed because he thought he should. Archie patted the bag.

We'll have double that in the next couple of weeks. Sean thought about a new life with ten grand. Archie patted the bag again.

But we've got a lot of work to do before then. Archie put the bag on the back seat.

Right, c'mon let's go.

Sean drove halfway back to the city centre and then Archie told him to pull over onto a lay-by that had a steep grass verge next to it.

Sean drove into the lay-by. At the top of the verge there was a wire fence and behind that a motor. He realised it was the same motor from the Fiveways car park. He turned off the engine and leaned back into his seat. Archie gave him directions for the delivery and told him what phone box he was to use when he'd picked up the parcel. When Sean repeated the instructions, Archie opened his door and got halfway out the motor.

And remember wee man, don't fuck this up.

Ah willnay Archie, Ah promise.

Archie looked at Sean, then pulled himself clear of the motor.

See ye in a wee while.

He slammed the car door and ran, bent forward, up the verge. He helped himself on by grabbing at the branches of shrubs. Five years in the prison gym powered him up the slope. At the top of the verge he vaulted the fence with one hand on a post. Then he stood by the motor and gave a salute that took Sean right back to their childhood. Archie turned around and got in the passenger seat and the motor screeched away before the door was shut. Sean wondered if he gave Sammy a row about his driving.

The homesteader gave his whip an exaggerated sweep and cracked it above the horses. The animals reared against the harnesses. The wagon bucked and started to roll. Dust cut through the smell of sweat and shit and smacked him on the face. He pulled his neckerchief over his mouth and his hat down over his eyes. It was going to be a hard ride. The people he was likely to meet would be bandits who had long lost any values taught to them by their God-fearing families. Get caught in an ambush by those bastards and the best he could hope for was a lingering death in the desert. From sunburn and thirst.

He drove towards the motorway. It darkened when the road curved under the M8 and the air hissed with the sound of cars flicking past concrete columns. He lit a fag while he was stuck at a set of lights. Before he was finished it, the carriageway twisted out and up to the left, away from the traffic lights and onto the motorway.

It was a thirty-minute journey to the service station. Long enough for him to go over the consequences.

They were drummed into his head by the rhythm of the tyres drumming over the concrete. He flew along the middle lane with them driving him on faster and faster.

*

After the polis nabbed me that night, Ah stopped doin the deliveries. But it was a fuckin nightmare. The family had got used to the money. Maggie liked her night out and the flatscreen telly. The wean liked her extra wee bits of pocket money and the sweeties Ah'd drop into her on a Saturday mornin. Try no doin that for a coupla weeks and they look at ye different. As if yer some sort of tight-arse. Ah could only take that treatment for so long. Before Ah knew what was happenin, Ah was back at Archie's door beggin for more bits of work.

And Ah wasnay just doin the one delivery a week. It was two or three. Ah'd drop parcels off and bring other ones back. Ah'd usually meet Archie in car parks. On the way home Ah'd have to phone him and he'd tell me where to go. Security is paramount he'd say, ye cannay be too careful in the drugs business. He couldnay insure against a snake in the grass.

Then it happened. Ah had just picked up a parcel and Ah got another tug. This time they knew what they were lookin for. Two motors pulled me into a lay-by and Gambo was in amongst them. He opened my car door and telt me to get out. Then he put his hand under the driver's seat and pulled out the parcel. What's this then? he said. Ah said Ah didnay know, it wasnay my motor. So he pulled me into one of the cop cars for a wee word.

Yer in trouble now Sean he said when the door was closed. Ah looked out the car window at the other coppers havin a fag and a wee laugh. Gambo telt me to look at him. Ah did and he went into one about the length of time Ah'd get when this got to court. He hadnay even opened the parcel. It was sat on his lap and he'd point to it now and again as if Ah'd forgotten it was there. He asked me if Ah was goin to take the rap for Archie. Ah shrugged my shoulders and telt him Archie was my brother, so what could Ah do?

But Gambo wasnay daft. He knew where to get me. He drew a wee picture of me lyin in a cell and Archie round mine lookin after the house. He'd already seen Archie call round while Ah was at work. Stayed for an hour or so, then he'd walked off down the road whistlin. Gambo had seen Archie look at Maggie and he'd seen that look a million times. As soon as Ah was safely away, Archie would be round mine cuttin the grass, and Maggie looks like the sort of woman that likes gettin her grass cut.

That's what done it. It wasnay all the batterins he'd gave me and the trouble with the polis. It was the fact that Ah knew he'd try and fuck her if he got half a chance. Ah couldnay have that. Ah mean, Maggie's a strong woman but there was no way Ah was goin to leave her at that cunt's mercy.

So Ah let Gambo follow me to the drop. When Ah got close, he hung back and waited for me to hand the motor back to my brother. Archie ran up when Ah pulled onto the car park. He jumped into the passenger seat. Everythin alright? he said. Ah telt him aye and he gave me my money. Ah got out and he slid into the driver's seat. He gave me a wave as he drove off. Ah watched him take the motor to the junction at the bottom of the street. That's where they jumped him. Last thing Ah heard was armed police and Ah was off like a sprinter. Straight over somebody's fence and through their garden.

Ah got to a phone box and telt Sammy what had happened. He said he'd sort things out and telt me to go home. And if the polis were to grab me, Ah was to say fuck-all. But that goes without sayin, know what Ah mean wee man? Ah said Aye and hung up. What else could Ah say?

*

Sean gripped the steering wheel tighter and bent forward to peer into the distance. Eventually a sign appeared.

Bothwell Services, that's the one.

He clicked the indicator down and pulled the car to the left-hand lane. Three two one and he was on the slip road and up and round and into the car park. The wagon bumped and shook as it slowed down in the car park. The homesteader had to keep his hand on his hat to make sure it didn't fall off. He kept his eye open for the silver Renault and there it was, with a black guy in the driver's seat. Sean pulled up beside it and rolled his window down. The black guy smiled.

Archie's brother. Yer his double.

Sean had only ever heard a Scouse accent on the telly. He reached out the window and they shook hands. The Scouser picked up a holdall and showed it to Sean.

That's your bag kid.

Sean held up the Tesco bag.

Cheers pal. Ah think this one's yours.

They swapped bags. The Scouser had a quick look in the Tesco bag, nodded to Sean and started up his motor.

Happy camping lad.

Sean nodded.

Safe journey home.

And you.

The Scouser wound up his window, lit a fag and turned his stereo on. As his car left the parking spot, he winked at Sean and was away.

Sean wrapped the strap round the holdall and put it on the floor behind the passenger seat, put his car in reverse.

Giddy up.

He watched the Scouser turn off for The South. Sean headed for Glasgow.

He rested back into his seat and flicked the harness with one hand. Acting casual like some fat businessman or grocery-store owner leaving Mexico for the north. He drove past one of them raised bits that the feds sit on to watch out for slavers and drug smugglers. There was a trooper sat on a horse. He had a cigar sticking out of his mouth and held a rifle across his horse's back. He had a long look at Sean as he swiped a fly away from his face. Sean didn't feel too safe. Sheriff Gambo's voice wouldn't count for much in this jurisdiction. No sir. This state trooper wouldn't care what the city police were up to. He'd be pleased to capture a man with a wagonload of contraband. So pleased he'd have a confession kicked out of Sean in no time flat. He'd still be wiping the blood from his hands as he placed his promotion application on the sergeant's desk.

But, safe or not, Sean didn't even blink. He kept his eyes on the horizon and tried to stay as cool as Steve McQueen. He didn't drive his wagon too fast. He didn't drive it too slow. He kept at an even pace. Straight down the centre of the highway. Heading for home with a couple of keys. He tipped his cowboy hat to the trooper to show he was grateful for the protection of the law. The trooper nodded back and Sean took a draw on his roll-up. He felt his neck go stiff with the effort of looking ahead.

The sweat was starting to dry by the time he saw the turn-off for Easterhouse. He looked in the mirror and indicated left. He swung round till he came to the traffic lights and took the next right. Then he looked out for the phone box. About two hundred yards Archie had said. And there it was, right next to a lay-by. He pulled in and turned the engine off. He checked behind the seat to make sure the holdall wasn't too visible. The last thing he needed was somebody to nick it while he was making the call. He got out the car, locked it, and went into the phone box. Archie answered after two rings.

Alright wee man?

Aye.

Ye should go and see Maggie's wee sister, she was askin for ye when Ah saw her earlier.

The phone went dead and Sean put the handset down. It seemed really obvious now. Lizzie lived just round the corner from here. It wouldn't take him five minutes to get there.

He stared at the phone. He took a couple of breaths. He picked it back up and made the call.

What's happenin?

Ah've got the gear and Ah've to drop it off to Archie.

Where?

Ah'll tell ye but Ah've got a condition.

There was a short silence before Gambo spoke.

What?

Let me get out of there before ye kick the doors in.

Ah'll do my best wee man.

Sean picked at a lighter burn in the phone box operating instructions. He didn't say anything.

Sean?

What?

Where are ye droppin the gear off?

Sean told him and hung up. He pushed his way out of the phone box and got back in the motor. He stretched the seat belt round his body and clicked it into place. He got his tobacco out and made a fag. The windows started to steam up and he realised Archie was waiting whether he wanted him to be or not. He tensed himself as he reached for the key and turned it until the starter coughed. He gave the accelerator a touch, pushed the clutch in and put the motor into gear. He looked over his shoulder and drew into the road.

After wiping his forehead he put his cowboy hat back on and took a long drink from his canteen. He checked his compass and rolled further into Bundy territory. He faced what he had to do with a steely glint in his eye. One slip and he was dead. All it would take would be a bead of sweat to run down his face as he was negotiating with the outlaws and his scrotum would become a valued tobacco pouch. Hopefully the quality of the goods would keep the outlaws dazzled enough for him to make an escape into the wilderness.

It only took half a cigarette for Sean to drive to Lizzie's. He parked the motor and grabbed the holdall out the back. He slung it over his shoulder and started walking up the path. A look up and down the street and he pushed into the close. It stunk of damp and piss. As he walked to the stairwell, he saw the orange cap from a syringe on the bottom step. The door creaked closed behind him as he climbed to the first floor.

A dirty nappy rested against the wall next to Lizzie's door. He banged the letterbox and a baby screamed inside the flat. Lizzie answered. She had the baby resting on her hip and a front tooth missing. Sean hadn't seen her in years but she didn't seem too interested in him. Her eyes scanned the lobby and the stairs but they always returned to the holdall. She jerked her head back into the flat and Sean followed her in.

Archie was on an easychair, with his fingers drumming the armrests. Sean showed him the bag. Archie grabbed it and put it between his legs.

Sammy.

Sammy came out of the kitchen and saw the holdall.

The man from Delmonte he say yeah.

Archie pulled a polythene package of gear out the holdall and put it on the coffee table. He cut into it with his Stanley and scooped a bit of powder onto the end of the blade. Lizzie looked like a broken dog eyeing a man with a steak. Archie nodded his head. She put the baby on the floor and went into the kitchen for a spoon. He tipped the gear into the spoon and she cooked up a hit. She gave herself the injection and fell back into the couch. Archie laughed.

A good bit of gear eh? Ye always get good stuff from the Scousers.

The baby cried and tugged at the legs of its mammy's jeans. Lizzie smiled and picked it up. The baby stopped screaming and nuzzled into her breast. Archie pointed at them.

Ah, mother and child. Is that no cute?

Sammy sniggered.

Fuckin junkie. Right, where's the good stuff?

Never mind that McCann, get on with sortin these out.

Sammy pulled another package of brown out of the bag and put it on the coffee table. He went into the kitchen and came back with a set of scales and a packet of freezer bags. He poured powder into the scales and tipped the pan into a freezer bag. Before long, he had a few packages sealed up on the table. Archie's phone rang and he pulled it out his pocket.

Aye no problem. Sammy'll run it round later.

Archie picked a smaller package out of the bag and put it on the coffee table. He cut into it and took out a bit of white powder and sniffed it up his nose. He looked at Sammy.

D'ye want a rock then son?

Sammy spoke out of the side of his mouth.

Does the Pope fuck weans?

Well get it together then.

Alright boss.

Archie smiled like a wife-beater indulging the wee woman in front of an audience.

And have less of the sarcasm.

Sammy went into the kitchen. He came back polishing a jam pot with a dirty tea towel. Archie put some of the charlie in the jar and sat it on the coffee table. He reached into his bag and brought out a squeezy bottle of ammonia. He pointed it at Sean.

Imagine this cunt in yer eyes?

Sean could.

Archie squirted some of the ammonia into the jar.

They didnay teach us this in school chemistry.

He passed the jar to Sammy.

Sort that out.

Sammy's eyes lit up when he grabbed the jar. He took it into the kitchen and Sean heard the microwave humming and pinging. Archie made an empty beer tin into a pipe. Sean looked at the living-room door and wondered when it would come crashing in.

Do ye need me any more?

No, but ye can stay for a pipe.

Ah would, but Ah want to get back home to Maggie.

Sammy called from the kitchen.

Under the thumb eh?

Sean looked at the kitchen door and Sammy came back through with some freshly prepared rocks.

Aye Sean, who's the boss in yer house? Check the state of him Archie. He's scared the wife'll gie him a row if he's out too long.

Archie looked at Sammy and narrowed his eyes. Then he looked at Sean.

Ah've never known ye to turn down a free pipe.

Ah just don't fancy it the night.

Aye, ma arse. What's goin on?

Sean couldn't keep his eye off the living-room door.

Fuck-all man.

Look at him Sammy. His eyes are all over the place. Sammy picked up the tin and started to pick through the rocks.

Fuck him. Ah want a pipe.

Archie stared at Sean for another few seconds, then looked at Sammy with the pipe.

No. Fuck the pipe. This cunt's up to somethin.

Sammy tutted and put it down. Sean started to sweat. Archie pointed at the couch.

Sit down.

Sean had another look at the living-room door and sat next to Lizzie. Sammy sat on the coffee table, looking at Sean. Archie leaned back and put his feet up.

So what's goin on?

Sean leaned forward and Sammy pushed him back into the couch. Lizzie snored and spluttered. Archie stood up.

Have ye seen that cunt Gambo lately?

Sean felt a fart moving around in his guts.

Gambo?

Archie walked over to the window and looked out.

Aye fuckin Gambo.

Sean tried to look all innocent.

Ah havenay saw him for donkey's years.

Archie sparked up a fag and walked back to the coffee table. He looked at Sean as he took a few puffs. Sean felt his head spin as he looked at his brother. The only sound in the flat was the *Coronation Street* theme tune from next door's telly. The ash fell from Archie's fag and landed on the carpet. He rubbed it in with his foot.

Sammy stood up.

Ah'm chokin for a fuckin pipe.

Archie looked at Sammy and shook his head.

Is that all ye think about?

Archie looked at Sean and had another puff on his fag. Smoke came out of his mouth as he spoke.

Tell ye what son. If there's somethin goin on, ye'll suffer.

Sean looked Archie in the eye.

Ah just want to get home to my wife.

Go on then. Fuck off.

Sean felt his hip click as he stood up. He straightened his jacket down over his waist.

Gie's a phone when ye need me.

Archie picked up the pipe.

Sean?

What?

Keys.

Sean took the car keys out of his pocket.

Ye couldnay gie's a tenner for a taxi home?

Archie pulled a tenner out and threw it at him.

Sammy, see him out. Make sure the door's locked when ye come back. Ye cannay trust no cunt on this scheme.

Archie lit the pipe and Sean saw his face change to that of a baby with a belly full of milk.

He walked out the flat and down the stairs. His footsteps echoed round the close with the clicks of the locks on Lizzie's front door. He pushed through the external doors and onto the front step. He had a breath of cold air and looked up the street. There was a car across the road with some men in it. He crossed the road and approached the car. In the passenger seat was Gambo. He rolled the window down as Sean approached.

Where is he?

In Lizzie's.

Is Sammy with him?

Aye.

What about the gear?

That's there as well.

Gambo nodded to the other policemen then turned back to Sean.

Good. Ye better toddle off home if ye don't want yer name mentioned in dispatches.

The police driver poked Gambo in the ribs with his elbow and pointed through the windscreen. Sean looked and saw a van pull up. Half a dozen policemen got out the back door. They stood in a circle while a sergeant made pointing gestures towards Lizzie's. Their breath cut into the night air. Another van drew up and the driver got a dog out of the back.

Sean went to say something, then changed his mind and walked down the street.

CHAPTER 16

The cold air bit into Sean's fingers. He had to turn his back on the wind to roll a fag. He lit it and turned and walked as he took his first draw. He put his hands in his pockets and walked with his head down and the fag hanging out the side of his mouth. He walked fast. Every time he heard a motor he stuck his thumb out for a lift. But no fucker stopped. They probably thought he was a junkie from the local scheme. A smelly bastard with dirty clothes. Nails that have been bitten till they hardly exist and teeth half-rotten and camouflaged with plaque. No wonder he didn't get a lift. They were scared in case he pulled a knife on them and took their wallets.

If somebody didn't stop soon, he'd die in this cold. It would be like one of them adverts for hypothermia. A guy staggers through a snowy waste. A voiceover tells the audience that one of the symptoms is a loss of coordination. In other words the guy looks like he's out of it. So the car drivers would fly past and have another reason to think Sean was a local junkie. Jesus. The poor guy was actually on his way to the graveyard. And nobody could tell. After a while he'd get really tired and decide to have a wee lie down. And the cars would still fly past, scared to stop. Next thing he's a frozen corpse and then every-body cares. The television crew come to the scene of misfortune. One of them presenters who looks like a social worker. Brown hair and the slight hint of a mous-tache. Her wee eyebrows would contract as she spoke into the microphone. The tragedy is that this poor man was lying here for three days before anyone thought to inform the relevant authorities. An unconfirmed police source said they would release the identity of the body when the relatives had been informed.

The big policeman would turn up at the door. One of the fat ones who can't handle arresting drunks and street gangs. When Maggie answered, he would put his hat under his arm. He'd nod and say something soft. She'd stand aside and he'd drag a nightmare into the house.

Sean took a draw on his fag and spat into the gutter.

At least Archie wouldnay be there he said to the cars. He pushed his head down and walked faster. Every time he heard a diesel engine he looked up in case it was a taxi. But there were just cars and vans and the odd lorry.

Eventually a black cab appeared on the horizon. It was travelling back the way Sean had come. The orange light was on. He stuck his hand in the air and waved. The taxi slowed and curved round the road till it stopped at his side. The cabbie reached across the front and pulled down the window.

Where ye goin pal?

Royston.

He had a good look at Sean.

Show's yer money.

Sean held up a tenner. The door clicked.

Get in.

He climbed in. His head hit the back seat as the cabbie dropped the clutch and they were away. He got his tobacco out and held it up to the eyes in the mirror.

Alright if Ah smoke?

Go ahead. Can ye can make me one as well?

Sean opened the pouch and pulled out his papers. There were only two left. He made the cigarettes and passed one to the front. The cabbie took it and sparked it up with a lighter he picked off the dashboard.

Cheers pal.

Sean sucked on his fag and blew the smoke against the window. He heard the driver cough.

Been out the night?

Just seein some pals.

Good night was it?

Sean rubbed a bit of ash off his trousers.

No bad Ah suppose.

Ah've had a few good nights up in Easterhouse myself. Ah remember one night about three years ago. Jesus. Ye should've seen the state Ah got in.

The taxi driver must have noticed Sean wasn't interested because he shut up and leaned into the steering wheel. Sean wondered if they'd managed to get Archie into the cells without any broken bones or bitten policemen. If they'd started questioning him. If they'd told him his brother had stuck him in.

★

Ah remember the time before when Ah grassed on him. The relief Ah felt when Ah knew he wouldnay be turnin up all the time lookin for favours or to stash stuff. For the first time in years me and Maggie had a Saturday night we could just sit in and enjoy. We got a coupla cans and watched the telly. The next mornin Maggie got up and made me fried eggs on toast and brought it back to the bed. Ah couldnay believe my luck.

About a year and a half into his sentence Donna came home from school with a leaflet about a trip the teachers had planned. It was a week in London takin in the sights and museums and art galleries. Maggie thought it would be good for the lassie, but it was goin to be dear. She telt Donna she didnay think we'd be able to afford it. Donna ran up the stairs greetin coz all her pals were goin. Me and Maggie just sat there lookin at each other, wonderin what we'd done wrong.

We had a talk about it. Ah thought, Ah might as well gie the school a bell to ask a bit about it. Her teacher said it would be a great opportunity for Donna. That it would show her the size of the world outside Royston and maybe encourage her to go to university when she was older. University Ah telt Maggie when Ah was finished with the call. She smiled and nodded and said university aye.

So what could Ah do but take the two hunner for the trip out of Archie's stash. It's only money Ah thought, and by the time he's back Ah'll have it replaced. Thing was, Maggie gied me the third degree about where the money came from. Ah telt her Ah'd won it at the bookies. She doesnay like me goin but she doesnay mind when Ah win.

Ye should've seen the look on Donna's face when Ah telt her. It was a picture. She jumped up and nearly broke my neck with a cuddle. Ah gied her fifty bar spendin money as well. Ah couldnay have her showed up in front of all her pals.

We waved her off on a single decker that drove out the school gates just as the sun was risin. Then Ah telt Maggie about the wee surprise Ah had for her. A holiday. A cheap one. Just the two of us for a weekend campin at the side of Loch Lomond. Ah'd took a lend of my uncle Albert's tent and that, and planked it in the house. It was a bit old but better than sleepin under the stars.

We just had to go home and pack up the stuff. A change of clothes. Some cans of beans, a loaf and a packet of ham. And half a dozen eggs. Then we jumped in a taxi to the bus station. A coupla hours on the bus and we were twistin through these country roads with the odd gleam of blue in the distance.

The bus dropped us near the camp site but it was still a fair hike to get to our pitch. It was good though. We could've been weans again on our first trip away the gether. Friday evening we pitched our tent and went to the chippy. After a good fish supper that was even tastier coz of the country air we bought a coupla bottles of cider and wandered down to the edge of the loch. We sat on a wall and watched the midges movin over the water. Ye'd see the odd splash as a fish jumped up tryin to grab one. My eyes filled with tears and Ah wished Ah had a pair of waders and Ah was out in the loch fly fishin like a fuckin lord. The sun was just on its way down and the sky reminded me of that time in Largs. It was beautiful.

Ah reached my hand round the back of Maggie's neck and pulled my fingers through her hair. She moved her head around and made a noise like she was eating the sweetest cake in the packet. She looked as beautiful as she was when she was seventeen.

When we'd drunk our cider we went back to the tent and Ah stood at the side and scratched my belly and had a piss while Maggie sorted the bed out. The midges were a bit cruel. But by the time we were all zippered up, and Ah'd killed a coupla the bastards that were inside, it was pure brilliant in there. We leaned back on our pillows and Maggie gied out a sigh. We had the torch stuck between our bodies and we did wee shadow puppets on the skin of the tent. The shadows started to get a bit saucy and the next thing Ah gied her a kiss. We ended up havin a shag and it was fuckin lovely. The best feelin Ah've ever had in my life. Even better than when Ah watched Donna gettin born.

Ah never wanted it to end. But it did.

Afterwards we lay there and Ah fell asleep with my cock still inside her. Ah woke up through the night and when Ah tried to stretch a bit my belly was unstuck from her back. Ah smelled her hair and felt my balls twinge ready for another go. She stretched a bit in her sleep and wiggled her arse and moaned.

But Ah heard a twig snap outside the tent and my cock went soft. Ah heard other noises like there was somebody outside the tent. Maybe it was a fox or somethin, but as Ah lay inside the tent Ah thought about a big jungle predator sneakin around lookin for prey and a shiver ran up my spine. Ah knew then that as long as Archie was alive we were never goin to have a chance at happiness.

★

The taxi braked and his head banged against the glass.

Whereabouts in Royston d'ye want?

Sean looked out and saw they were nearly there. He scratched his head.

Just drop us at the bottom of Cadge Road.

What, the Royston Road end?

Aye that'll be brilliant.

The taxi stopped at a traffic light and he thought he saw a flake of snow in the air. Then he saw another one. He sat up and looked out the front of the cab. He seen the odd flake dancing around the headlights. They were that small he could be imagining them. The cabbie tutted.

Looks like we're in for another night of snow.

Sean nodded.

Aye. Ah'm sick of it already.

The taxi turned into Royston Road and Sean looked out the window. Orange snow swirled round the street lights. The driver put on his windscreen wipers.

There ye go pal, nearly there.

Aye thanks. Saved me a rough walk the night.

Whereabout?

Sean remembered he had no fag papers left.

Just drop me at the off-licence.

The taxi stopped and the guy turned round.

Nine pound.

Sean gave him the tenner and waved away the change. He got out and slammed the door. He pulled his jacket around himself and watched the red lights of the cab disappear into the night.

He went into the shop. It was like walking into a cage with a hatch built-in to pass the drink through. A Pakistani guy stood smoking behind the counter. Sean nodded to him.

Some weather we've been havin.

The guy leaned against the cage.

Aye it's unreal. But what do ye expect for January?

Yer right enough.

What can Ah get ye?

Two packets of green Rizla.

The guy reached under the counter and slapped them on the counter.

Forty pence.

Sean put the money on the counter and put the papers in his tobacco pouch.

Cheers pal.

Go easy on the way home.

Sean pulled the door open and stepped onto the pavement. It was windy and the snow was whipped up the street like sand in the desert. He started the march home.

Sergeant O'Grady was miles away from a snare drum yet he could still hear it rattle in his head, keeping time, making sure his boots clicked the pavement at an even pace. His shoulder ached under his kitbag but he knew if he put it down he'd have to go through the agony of stretching out his arm. He straightened his back and kept on moving. His medal-laden chest had faced the flashing swords of Indian tribesmen, the assegais of Zulu warriors, and the razors of Italian whores. The walk up Cadge Road was nothing next to these exploits, but it was going to be a cold march.

For one thing, his kilt didn't keep him very warm. His legs were almost blue and covered in goose bumps. Forebears of his had marched all over the Highlands dressed like this with hardly a shiver. Sleeping out in the heather with a bit of tartan wrapped round their skinny bodies then up at dawn for a battle with the English. But Sergeant O'Grady was used to warmer climates. Jungles where the itch from leech bites made a man wish he was dead. Deserts where his lips cracked and his tongue felt like a piece of paper. And cities he had smelled before they appeared on the horizon.

He was tired of war. All he wanted was to go home and warm his legs by the fire, and have his missus and daughter sat on the couch beside him.

Sergeant O'Grady stood by his garden gate and sniffed the air. He was sure he could smell a touch of smoke in the wind. It worried him, but maybe it was just a trace of the last battle lodged somewhere in his nose. He looked up and down the street before pushing the gate open and walking up the path.

Chapter 17

Maggie helped him off with his jacket and hung it on the post at the bottom of the stairs. He rubbed his hands together.

Are ye makin us a cup of tea then or what?

She walked past him into the kitchen, picked up the kettle and turned to face him.

So what happened?

He pulled a chair out and sat down by the table. He drummed his fingers on his knee as he told her.

Thank Christ for that she said.

He leaned forward and put his face in his hands. He heard her fill the kettle and put it on. Then he felt her warm hands on his neck.

Ye've done the right thing love.

Ah fuckin hope so.

Her hands rubbed his neck as the kettle boiled.

Was my sister there?

Aye. She looked fucked.

Stupid cow. Ah suppose she'll get the jail as well?

Aye.

Was there a lot of drugs?

Enough for the whole of Glesga to have a party.

The kettle boiled and she took her hands from his neck. She made the tea and sat at the other side of the table. Sean had a sip. It burned the tip of his tongue.

This is fuckin roastin.

Ye'd be complainin if it was cold.

Ha fuckin ha.

Maggie smiled and pulled open her fag packet. She offered him one. He took it.

He'll get a few years this time.

She reached across the table and laid her hands on top of Sean's.

Ah'm really proud of ye.

He looked at his wife and felt like crying. He pulled his hand away from her and rested his forehead on it as he had another draw on his fag. She stood up and took their mugs to the sink. She rinsed them out and put them on the drying rack. She walked to the press and grabbed a tea towel.

Ah might as well dry these.

Sean turned and grasped her leg and pulled her close.

Just leave them for now.

He pulled her onto his lap and pushed his head into her chest. Maggie put her arms round his shoulders and he felt her chest rise with her breath. He picked her necklace up with his mouth and sucked the end of it. She stroked his head.

Albert phoned a wee while ago.

Sean kept sucking the necklace.

He wanted to know where ye were.

Sean dropped the necklace.

What did ye tell him?

Ah just said ye had something to sort out with Archie. Ye could gie him a bell.

Ah'll talk to him the morra.

He picked the necklace back up with his lips. They sat like that for a while before she got up and grabbed his hand.

C'mon through to the livin room.

Ah'll just take my trainers off. Be through in a minute. Maggie left the kitchen. Sean sat and stared at the curtains. They had the same pattern as a pair his mammy had.

★

Ah was happy when me and Archie went to school that mornin coz it was giro day. Ah knew when we got home there would be a decent dinner for a change and my da would be in a good mood. Ah spent half the day at school tellin everybody what Ah was goin to do with ma pocket money when Ah got it.

But when we got home there was no big dinner. Our ma was sittin at the kitchen table. She was drinkin Eldorado out of her blue and white striped mug. We asked for our pocket money and she telt us we were selfish wee bastards. Just like him she said, and started greetin. Our da had went tae the post office in the mornin but he hadnay came back. Archie asked where he was. She didnay fuckin know she telt him, and put her head on her arms on the table.

Ah went over tae gie her a cuddle and she telt me

to fuck off. Ah said but Mammy and she gied me a skelp on the side of the head. Her weddin ring caught me on the cheek and dug right into my skin. Then she was greetin again, goin Ah'm sorry son and cuddlin and kissin me. The smell of drink of made me want to be sick.

She went into the livin room and sat in front of the telly. Archie made me a piece on brown sauce and telt me he was goin to Uncle Albert's and Ah was to stay with our ma. Ah didnay want to but Ah did as Ah was telt. Ah ended up sittin in the livin room watchin her from my da's chair. It was fuckin crazy. One minute she was callin me all the bastards and sayin it was my fault my da had fucked off. Then the next she was sayin sorry, she should be struck down for talkin like this to her youngest wean.

She staggered over and cuddled me and Ah squirmed away from her kisses. She telt me Ah was the double of my da and he wouldnay run away and leave his weans. No he wouldnay do that. She shook her head and dried her eyes. Sniffed and wiped round her nose and said it again. No he wouldnay leave his weans. Then she looked at the clock and started greetin again. Where the fuck are ye? She went back to her chair and picked up her fags. She lit one and sucked the smoke into herself as if it was the soul of my da. Then she stood up and went to the window. Where the fuck are ye Paddy?

By the time Archie came back with my uncle Albert, she'd finished the Eldorado and was fallin asleep on the couch with a fag droopin in her fingers. Albert looked at her and tutted. Archie picked the fag from her hand

and stubbed it out in the ashtray. Then they grabbed an oxter each and dragged her upstairs to her bed. When they were comin back down, Ah heard her howlin ye cannay leave me no like this.

Albert took us to his house. He pulled the cushions off the couch and made Archie a bed on the floor. Ah got to sleep on the couch.

When we were wrapped up in the blankets, he came through to tuck us in. He put his hand on my head and telt me and Archie no to worry about our ma and da. It'll get sorted out boys, don't worry about that. Then him and my auntie went into the kitchen. Jessie telt Albert that my da was a fuckin waster. Albert telt her to shut it in case the weans were listenin. She said they'd have to hear it one day so it might as well be now. Albert shut the door and all Ah heard after that was the rumble of his voice through the wall. Then the kettle whistled and Ah must have fell asleep, coz the next thing Ah knew it was the mornin.

My auntie Jessie filled us up with porridge and took us to school. She picked us up that night as well. We ended up stayin with them for a week before we could go back home. It was alright round there. Ye got a big dinner every night and a chocolate biscuit for afters. Ye even got the odd two bob for sweeties at school.

But when we went back home, my da still wasnay there.

We never saw him again. About a year after he fucked off, we were sittin down to our dinner and my ma started greetin. She blurted out that he'd ran away to London with some woman from Paisley. They were stayin in a bed and breakfast in Soho. My ma said she hoped the lassie broke my da's heart like he'd broke hers. She said it was fuckin tragic that we were two wee boys to grow up without a father to look after them, and him runnin about London with hoors and drunks. She didnay know how we were goin to cope. She telt us my da was nothin but a selfish bastard and hell could fuckin mend him as far as she was concerned. Me and Archie looked at each other and got on with our dinner.

*

Maggie came back into the kitchen.

So there ye are.

He kicked off his trainers and she took them into the lobby. She came back through with his slippers and he put them on. They went into the living room. He sat on the couch and she turned the telly on. He put his feet up on the coffee table. She went to the kitchen and appeared with a can of beer. He took it and sparked it open. She sat next to him and snuggled in against his body. They sat back and watched the telly.

There was a programme on about this Australian guy who wrestles with dangerous creatures. It was set in the outback. The guy had a pair of shorts on and he was circling round this big snake. He said it was one of the most poisonous reptiles in the world. The poor wee thing was trying to get away from him but the guy would run round and try and pick it up by the tail. Maggie shook her head.

That's cruel, that is.

But the guy on the telly didn't hear her. He eventually got hold of its tail and picked it up. It twisted and turned trying to get a bite into him. The guy said when their heads go into an S shape, that's when you have to worry. After a while the snake seemed to give up and just hung from his hand. It was defeated and wanted to go off somewhere quiet for a bit of mouse or whatever it is they eat. But the guy wasn't finished with it. He shook it a bit and danced round with it. Then it went into the S shape. It started to hiss. The guy said it was really angry now and he'd have to be careful because the species is known to do multiple bites. He put it back on the grass. The snake tried to slither away and the guy bent down and crawled after it. He was coming out with all this Australian talk. There you go mate. Yer all right now fella. Sean looked at Maggie.

Ah hope it turns and bites the cunt on the snout.

The phone rang and Sean flinched. Maggie got up and answered it. Sean heard the rumble of a man's voice on the other end. Maggie held the phone towards him.

It's Gambo for you.

Her face looked white. He picked up the phone.

Sean?

Aye.

Bad news.

Sean felt like he'd had a hard punch in the guts. He knew what was coming.

What?

He got away.

Are ye fuckin kiddin? How the fuck did that happen?

He jumped out the kitchen window.

And ye didnay have anybody coverin the backs?

They were all needed at the front door.

But ye had a van full of polis.

Gambo never said anything. Sean looked out the side of the curtains at the snowy night.

So where does that leave me?

There was a pause before Gambo answered.

Just keep yer doors locked.

What? Is that it?

Well what d'ye want me to do about it?

Send somebody round.

We cannay spare anybody Sean. We've got the others to question, and anyway it's Friday night. We're snowed under with fuckin drunks.

Aye yer a busy man.

Nay need for sarcasm.

It's alright for you to say. Ah'm the one that's got to deal with Archie.

All ye need to do is keep yer doors locked. If he turns up, gie's a phone. We'll get to ye within a quarter an hour.

That's reassurin.

Just don't let the cunt in yer house.

The phone went dead. Sean slammed it down. He looked at Maggie as she sat on the edge of the couch.

They've fucked that up. Stupid bastards.

She nodded. He could see she was scared. She looked up at him.

What are we goin to do?

Sergeant O'Grady looked round with the eye of a

practised warrior. They had no rifles or gunpowder. Just sticks and knives. But he'd fought through tougher odds than this. The communication wire was intact. All they had to do was secure the gates to the fort and, when the enemy arrived, call for reinforcements.

We better make sure this place is battened up. Get the front door. Ah'll check the back.

Maggie stood up and he walked behind her into the hall. She went to the door and tested the mortise. Then she slid the bolt across and put the chain on.

Sean looked at her wee body struggling with the locks. He sighed and went through to the back lobby. When he got there, a draught whipped the kitchen door out of his hands and slammed it closed. He almost shat himself and a flush of goose pimples ran up his back. It was freezing cold in there. He tutted and shook his head when he saw the key was in the lock.

That's askin to get burgled, so it is.

He reached up to pull it out when a tattooed fist smashed through the window and turned the key. Sean grabbed the wrist and twisted it round the window frame. Blood flowed as it caught on the bits of broken glass. Then the wrist pulled back out and Sean let go. He pushed against the door and tried to lock it. But Archie had already started ramming it and the key wouldn't turn.

Sir, sir.

Yes Dogby?

He's coming sir, he's coming.

Discipline Dogby, there's a good chap.

Sergeant O'Grady used the weight of his shoulders

to hold the line against the enemy. He called for his men to back him up. He rallied them on as he motioned forward with his pistol. But the door kept springing open. It was as if there was a mass of soldiers outside slamming it with the trunk of an oak tree. Defenders on the roof threw grenades which sent assailants screaming to the floor. But there were plenty of willing replacements. Sergeant O'Grady was tired. He'd never fought against such a tenacious foe. He used every inch of his strength. He shouted and pointed his gun at his men. But they were so fatigued, they didn't care if they died.

Sean felt his wife push behind him. He could hear her desperate wee grunts every time Archie charged. The door bounced with the power of a cannon. Every recoil weakened him and his body sagged further to the floor.

Archie managed to squeeze between the door and the jamb. Sean pushed with the strength of the desperate. But even with Maggie behind him, it wasn't enough. He tried to make a wedge with his body but his feet slid on the lino. Archie got enough of himself inside so that his arm could swing freely. He punched Sean on the side of the head. Every time Sean tried to avoid a punch, he could feel Archie snake more of his body into the gap. Archie's fist banged him harder and harder until Sean knew he was defeated and let go. The force pushed him and Maggie to the floor.

Archie entered the house with his chest puffed up like an angry tiger. He drew his sleeve across his sweaty forehead. Snow melted from his hair and landed on his jacket. He looked down at the couple struggling to get up.

What were ye no lettin me in for?

Sean didn't know what to say. Archie bent down and punched him on the chest.

Ya fuckin wee prick.

Sean could hardly take a breath as he lay on the floor. He lifted his head and watched Archie swagger into the kitchen. The bad bastard pulled some dishes off a worktop. They shattered as they hit the floor. He spat in the sink and turned to face them. Maggie followed him with her hand on her hips like a wee soldier.

What d'ye think yer doin, bargin into my house?

What the fuck are ye goin to do about it?

Sean got up and went into the kitchen. He stood next to Maggie. Archie moved his head like a weightlifter loosening up his neck. But all the time he stared into Sean's eyes. His arms were at his side and blood ran down his hand and dripped off the end of his finger onto the lino. He didn't seem to notice. Sean pointed at the blood.

Ye've cut yer hand.

Archie lifted it up and looked at it. He put it back down.

So fuckin what?

Ye'll bleed to death said Maggie.

Archie laughed.

Shut up ya stupid hoor.

Maggie went into the airing cupboard and took out a tea towel.

Let me sort out yer arm.

Archie held his wrist in his hand.

Fuck off.

She threw the tea towel on the table.

Please yerself, but it's there if ye want it.

He grabbed it and pressed it to his wrist. He looked at Sean.

Why d'ye stick me in?

Sean shook his head.

Ah never.

Archie lips curled. He whispered.

Grass.

Ah swear on it.

Archie kicked one of the chairs so hard it broke.

Yer a lyin cunt.

Maggie went to the kettle.

Why don't yeez both calm down and Ah'll make some tea.

Archie looked at her. He breathed a couple of times through his nose.

Two sugars and milk.

Archie pointed to a chair next to Sean.

Sit down.

Sergeant O'Grady felt the rope dig into his wrists as he sat in the circle of prisoners. He knew there was nothing to look forward to but a short tortured life before he joined the half of his platoon that were already dead. He sat with his back straight and looked the chief savage in the eye. The savage growled.

What the fuck are ye lookin at?

Sean realised he was on his own. He took his eyes from his brother and settled them on the curtains. Archie nodded to Maggie.

Sit down.

Maggie stayed standing up. Archie sat down across the table from Sean.

Go on hen, take the weight off yer feet.

Maggie sat down. Archie grabbed a fag out of her packet and lit up. He nodded at the packet.

Ye don't mind, do ye?

Maggie folded her hands over her stomach.

What d'ye want?

Archie took a long slow draw on his fag before he nodded at Sean.

Why don't ye ask that cunt?

The kettle started to boil. Archie nodded at Maggie.

Are ye makin that tea then or what?

Maggie got up and went to the worktop. Archie took a long drag on his cigarette and nodded after Maggie.

What are ye doin with this prick? Ye could have a better life with a real man.

Maggie didn't even turn round.

Ah've got a real man.

Archie flicked ash on the table.

Sure ye have doll.

He pointed his fag at Sean.

So why did ye do it?

Ah don't know what yer talkin about.

He gave Sean the disappointed look Albert used to give them when they were children. Then he took a puff and smiled and nodded.

Are ye havin a fag?

Sean reached across the table and Archie grabbed his hand. He felt his knuckles click together and Archie's nails dig right into his skin. He tried to pull his hand away but Archie held it fast. Archie stared into Sean's eyes.

Why the fuck did ye grass me up?

Sean knew what was coming and struggled to get away but he was held tight. He got up off the chair and had nearly twisted free when Archie crushed the fag into the soft part of his wrist. He screamed.

Ah didnay want to do it.

Archie let him go and he pulled his burnt wrist to his mouth. Maggie shouted at Archie.

What the fuck are ye playin at?

She pushed Sean to the sink and ran cold water on his freshly branded arm. He looked over his shoulder at his brother.

Archie twirled the broken cigarette between his fingers and threw it to the floor. He stood up like a workman with a job to do and sauntered over to the sink. He put his hand on Maggie's chest and pushed her out of the way. He grabbed Sean by the tee shirt. Sean felt his chest hairs being pulled out as his shirt was twisted round Archie's fist. Their faces were so close they touched noses. Spittle flew from Archie's teeth as he spoke in a loud whisper.

Ah'm goin to fuckin kill ye ya wee cunt.

The edge of the sink unit dug into his back as Archie pushed him against it. Sean flinched as he waited for the worst kicking in his life. Out of the corner of his eye he saw Maggie holding up a mug.

D'ye no want yer tea Archie?

Archie turned to her.

Stick it up yer arse.

Maggie threw the tea into his face. He roared and put his hands up too late to protect himself. He shook his head like a boxer trying to blink the sweat out of his eyes. Tea dripped off his chin and onto his jacket.

There was a moment of stillness before he pounced. He ricocheted off the table and the cooker on his way to his target. She was forced into the corner before he got his hands round her neck. He lifted her up and shook her so hard her feet banged against the wall.

Ya dirty fuckin slut.

Sean gripped the back of Archie's jacket and tried to drag him off. The big bastard didn't stop throttling Maggie. Sean looked round and saw a knife amongst the dishes at the side of the sink. He snatched it up, and with an over-handed arc sunk it into his brother's back. Archie grunted and bucked, but he still didn't let go. Maggie coughed like a dying woman. Sean gripped the collar of the jacket and jerked the knife free. He pulled the denim down as hard as he could and stabbed into the unprotected neck. He stabbed and stabbed till Archie slumped like a battleship in a frothing sea of blood. Sean backed away as the big man hit the floor.

Ya dirty cunt ye.

Maggie started to speak but just coughed some more. She rubbed her throat and tried to stand up. Sean stepped over Archie, took her by the wrist, and pulled her upright. He stroked tears from her cheeks with his thumb.

Are ye alright?

She nodded and wrapped her arms round him.

Sean held the back of her head as he looked at his brother.

Ah've fucked it now.

Archie twitched like a baby falling asleep.

SAMSON

DAVID MAINE

Samson, every Sunday school's favourite mass murderer, wreaks havoc whenever he or his Lord have been challenged. But every hard man has a soft spot. And when Samson meets Dalila, he finds a woman who changes everything . . .

David Maine's latest novel is a magnificent piece of storytelling and a fable for our times.

'Racy and entertaining.' *Guardian*

'A blistering and provocative portrait of someone more akin to God's own gangster than God's gift to mankind.' *Time Out*

£7.99

ISBN 978 1 84767 042 7

BONE IN THE THROAT

ANTHONY BOURDAIN

All is not well at the Dreadnought Grill. The chef's on drugs, the owner's been set up by the FBI and, despite all this, sous-chef Tommy is just trying to do his job. As depraved as it is hilarious, Anthony Bourdain's first novel is spiced with foul-mouthed Feds, salty mob speak and a cast of unforgettables.

'Raw and cooking. Rare and well-done.' AA Gill

'A superb tale of violence and back-biting set in the seething testosterone-heavy company of a crew of New York cooks.' *GQ*

£6.99

ISBN 978 1 84767 054 0

GRAFFITI MY SOUL

NIVEN GOVINDEN

This is Surrey, where nothing bad ever happens. Except somehow, 15-year-old Veerapen, half-Tamil, half-Jew and the fastest runner in school, has just helped bury Moon Suzuki, the girl he loved. His dad has run off with an optician and his mum's going off the rails. Since when did growing up in the suburbs get this complicated?

'A sharp update on *Catcher in the Rye*.' *Arena*

'Outstanding . . . You become totally immersed. A powerful social commentary.' *Independent on Sunday*

£7.99

ISBN 978 1 84767 097 7

BORN FREE

LAURA HIRD

Shortlisted for the Whitbread First Novel Award

Punchy, sharp-witted and acutely observed, *Born Free* tells the story of an ordinary family who are all trying to escape from something . . . and each other. The voices of Jake, Joni, Angie and Vic reveal a hellish cocktail of adolescent and mid-life crises, savage sibling rivalry, a marriage gone cold – and naturally, the unbridgeable gap between generations. It's a story of everyday life.

'Desperately readable, blackly comic and painful, a delight born of dysfunction.' *The Times*

£7.99

ISBN 978 1 84195 048 8

GOLD

DAN RHODES

From the bestselling author of *Timoleon Vieta Come Home*

Miyuki Woodward goes on holiday to the same village every year. The locals are especially glad of her trivia prowess during pub-quiz nights; but, this year, Miyuki will take part in the most turbulent events the village has ever seen. Tear-inducingly funny and unputdownable, *Gold* is a novel about love and belonging.

'Absolutely flawless. Original, fresh and funny.' *Observer*

'Hilarious and acutely affecting.' *Independent on Sunday*

£7.99

ISBN 978 1 84767 048 9

WHEN TO WALK

REBECCA GOWERS

It looks like just another week ahead. Then out of the blue Ramble's husband ends their marriage over lunch and disappears. She is forced to reconsider everything she's ever been taught by her screwy relatives, unreliable friends and wayward criminal connections. Should she hide in life's slipstream, or has the moment come to break free?

'As darkly funny as Sylvia Plath and as eccentric as George Saunders. Gowers is a genius.' Scarlett Thomas

£7.99

ISBN 978 1 84767 043 4